You just need that extra kick

冤家英語DD

陳幸美◎著

每天冤一下，英語才未散！

冤家英語的四「不」一「沒有」

四「不」

✗ 不帶「髒」字的吵架，才能堪稱是最上乘的吵架

✗ 不令人討厭又準確傳達出最高意境

✗ 不再瞎子摸象，書中四大情境show you how！！！

✗ 不再玻璃心，邊吵邊強化心智，更磨練自己的英文

一「沒有」

✗ 沒有其他選擇，看這本就對了，
好好practice吧！你就是吵架王！！！

MP3

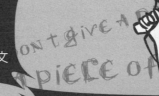

作者序
Author's Preface

到 人生地不熟的國家，發生問題的時候只能靠自己。結結巴巴，詞不達意，就只有『囧』字可以形容。記得當年是從一個對出國充滿美好幻想的高職畢業生，出了國門才驚覺原來從現在開始出了事就要自己處理。為了克服語言障礙，以不怕丟臉的態度，逐漸地融入當地社會，澳洲也成了第二個家。

綜合筆者本身的人生體驗，將《冤家英語》分成四個章節。以不同角色可能會遇到的狀況作區隔，配合口語的方式來撰寫，各種窘境都能輕鬆應對。有句話說：成為有經驗的人是來自壞經驗的累積，而壞經驗是因為本身沒有經驗。(Good experience comes from bad experience and bad experience comes from inexperience.)希望讀者看完這本書之後，能夠體驗書裡的壞經驗而變得有自信、有能力處理突發狀況。

陳幸美 Josephine Merrett

編者序
Editor's Preface

許多人常會有種感覺，考了許多英文檢定，念了許多英文，考試但看歐美影集或外國頻道卻像鴨子聽雷，或是到國外求學、澳洲打工面對許多生活情景類的問題時，卻無法適切表達自己的看法。不知道如何跟教授解釋作業無法如期寫完的原因、選課錯誤該如何處理、有租屋問題等不知道該如何反應。或是自助旅行時遇到想取消訂房、看醫生卻沒有保險、機場退稅時遇到一些狀況，講不出個所以然。這些溝通問題更常發生於有交外籍男或女友的友人中，時常在回過神後，思考著那你／妳怎麼會這樣回答，難怪彼此溝通會產生誤會，或對話對方會聽不懂囉。

這本書綜合了留學生、外派人員、上班族、異國情侶、背包客、觀光客會遇到的情境，從活潑生動的吵架情境中相信你可以迅速汲取英文生活用語而收穫良多。

編輯部 敬上

目次
CONTENTS

PART 01
留學生與外派人員

PART 02
上班族

PART **03**
異國情侶

篇章回顧 ❸

PART 04
背包客和觀光客

PART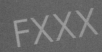

留學生與外派人員

學習進度表

- [ ] 1. 機場接機
- [ ] 2. 註冊費遲交
- [ ] 3. 選課錯誤
- [ ] 4. 銀行開戶
- [ ] 5. 作業要求延期交件
- [ ] 6. 科目被當見教授
- [ ] 7. 買學生票沒帶證件
- [ ] 8. 宿舍室友吵鬧
- [ ] 9. 共用廚房誰整理
- [ ] 10. 房屋修繕
- [ ] 11. 退租押金
- [ ] 12. 安裝電話費用的紛爭
- [ ] 13. 買車
- [ ] 14. 車窗被砸
- [ ] 15. 預約看醫生
- [ ] 16. 有人插隊
- [ ] 17. 申請表填錯
- [ ] 18. 上網購物收到錯誤商品

看完的單元也別忘了打勾喔！！

Unit 1 機場接機

前情提要

Mark 在前往美國留學之前已經事先請代辦中心安排好接機的服務，可是到了機場發現並沒有人來接機，因時差的關係無法聯絡上台灣的代辦中心所以打電話到接機服務中心要求他們派人來接。接機中心表示早上已經派人去過機場但沒接到人。**Mark** 行前的確更改過機位，但已有通知代辦中心。**Mark** 現在被卡在機場，他要求派司機回來接他。

人物角色

- Mark 留學生
- Customer service 接機服務中心的客服人員

情境對話　　　MP3 01

Customer service: I am afraid all our drivers are **flat out** at the moment. I would suggest you take a taxi

客服：很抱歉我們司機現在都很忙。我建議您自己搭計程車到學校，可是車

from the airport to the campus, but it would cost you **an arm and a leg.**

Mark: Would you refund the cost of the pickup service since I was not picked up?

Customer service: Unfortunately, it has all been prepaid, and it is customer's responsibility to provide us the correct flight details.

Mark: That is totally unfair! I did provide the correct itinerary to my agent. It is not my fault if the information somehow got **lost in the system. I can't get hold of** my agent due to the time difference. If I would be charged anyway, I **would rather stick around** here for your next available driver.

費會很貴。

馬克：那你會退我接機的費用嗎？畢竟沒有人來接我啊。

客服：恐怕不行，因為接機服務都是預付的，而且提供正確的行程表是客人的責任。

馬克：這真是太不公平了，我有通知代辦中心我更改了機位，你們沒有收到正確的訂位紀錄不是我的錯。因為時差的關係我聯絡不上代辦中心。如果你們堅持要收費的話，那我情願等你們的司機有空。

01 留學生與外派人員

02 上班族

03 異國情侶

04 背包客和觀光客

慣用語

1. flat out　忙壞了

I am **flat out** here, do you think you can give me a hand when you are done?

我忙到爆，如果你做完可不可以來幫我一下

---

2. an arm and a leg　很貴

A decent diamond ring could cost you **an arm and a leg**.

好得鑽戒可是貴得很

---

3. lost in the system　搞丟了

I never seem his application form, I guess it got **lost in the system**.

我從未看過他的申請表，應該是系統沒存到。

---

4. get hold of　找尋

Do you know where Jason is? I have been trying to **get hold of** him.

你知道傑森去哪裡嗎？我一直在找他。

---

5. would rather　我情願

I **would rather** pay for the taxi than waiting in the airport for another hour.

我情願自己付計程車的錢也不要在機場再等一小時。

6. **stick around**　留下來，等待

Would you **stick around** and keep me accompany? I am a bit scared.

你留下來陪我好嗎？我有一點害怕。

---

7. **waste of time**　浪費時間

I don't know how long I have to sit here for. It is just a **waste of time**.

我不知道我還要在這裡等多久，真的很浪費時間。

---

8. **in the queue**　排隊

Sorry for the delay, I was stuck at the custom; there are lots of people **in the queue**.

抱歉我出來晚了，我卡在海關，因為有很多人在排隊。

Memo

Unit 2 ‧ 註冊費遲交

 前情提要

　　Cathy 半年前到美國就讀大學，這學期她的學費是由台灣的父母直接匯到學校帳戶。但在開學後收到學校的通知說註冊費遲繳需付罰金 200 美金，Cathy 決定要到註冊處去問清楚。

人物角色

● Cathy 留學生
● Sally 收銀員

情境對話 MP3 02

Cathy: Hi, I received this letter stating I have to pay additional 200 dollars for the delayed student fee.

凱西：您好，我收到這封信說我的註冊費遲繳，要多交 200 美金的遲交罰金。

Sally: Well, you got that right! The tuition was late by the 2 days. Unfortunately, if you wish to avoid the late fee, you got to be **in time**.

Cathy: That is unreasonable. You got to understand I am an international student and my fees are wire transferred directly into the school account from overseas. My parents definitely did it before the deadline; however, we **have no control of** when the money would reach the school account. I can show you the bank receipt as the **proof of payment** it was done before the deadline. I think it should be sufficient enough for the late fees to **be waived**.

收銀員莎莉：你說對了，你的學費晚了兩天入帳。很遺憾地，如果你不想被罰錢的話，就要及時繳交。

凱西：這不合理，你要知道我是留學生，我的學費是從國外直接電匯到學校的帳戶。我爸媽真的是在期限前去電匯的，只是我們無法控制要花多長的時間錢才會入帳。我有銀行水單可以做憑證，學費是在期限前匯的。這樣應該可以免去遲繳罰金了吧！

 慣用語

1. in time 及時

Thank God the pay cheque arrived **in time**, otherwise I would be stuck with no money at all.

還好薪水及時入帳了，不然我真的一毛錢都沒有。

---

2. have no control of 無法控制

Not all places would cash traveller's cheque for you. That is something you **have no control of**.

並不是每個地方都願意收旅行支票。這點你就沒有辦法控制。

---

3. proof of payment 付款證明

I should have kept the receipt as **proof of payment**. I might have to look itup from my bank statement now.

早知道我應該把收據留下來當付款證明，現在我可能要查一下我的銀行對帳單。

---

4. Be waived 免付，刪除費用

The advertisement says the account keeping fee **is waived** for the first two years.

廣告上說頭兩年免付帳戶管理費。

---

5. One click away 只要上網處理

Why don't you register as one of our online banking customer? You can handle all the transactions with only **one click away**.

為什麼不註冊成為我們的網路銀行會員呢？所有的交易都可以上網處理。

---

6. **At your convenience**　**你方便的時候**

Once you got the online banking password, you can pay your tuition **at your convenience.**

等你收到網路銀行的密碼後，你方便時就可以登入付學費。

---

7. **Hassle-free**　**省事、輕易的**

Next time you can get a money order from the post office. It is **hassle-free**.

下次你可以直接到郵局買匯票，那很容易。

---

8. **From now on**　**從現在開始、以後**

I think I will start saving up for the tuition of next year **from now on**.

我想我應該從現在開始存明年的學費。

Unit 3 選課錯誤

🌸 前情提要

　　Johnny 和朋友在討論選課的內容，Johnny 突然發現他選錯課了，而他應該要選的那門課已經額滿了，他只好硬著頭皮去教務處找人幫忙。

👤 人物角色

- ◉ Johnny 留學生
- ◉ Mr. Larson 教務處人員

👄 情境對話　　　　MP3 03

Johnny: I am sorry that I **screwed this up**, how could I have not realized Marketing 101 is the pre-requisite for Advance Marketing? I have **pulled out** from Advance Marketing,

強尼：我很抱歉我搞砸了，我怎麼會不知道行銷學 101 是進階行銷學的基礎課程。我已經取消進階行銷學的選課了，可是行

but all the Marketing 101 classes are full.

Mr. Larson: This happens every semester. It was mentioned **over and over**, but no one **pays any attention** on what we said. Unfortunately there is nothing I can do at this moment, your **best bet** would be waiting for someone to drop this unit and hopefully you can **take over** the spot. Otherwise you would have to wait for next semester then.

Johnny: Please do your best to **squeeze me in**; otherwise, I would have to **put off** the graduation for another 6 months.

銷學 101 的課全是滿的。

拉森先生：這種事怎麼每個學期都發生，我們說了又說可是都沒有人聽進去。很可惜地目前我幫不上你忙，最好的方式就是等開學後有人要退選，希望你可以填上那個空缺，不然你就只好等下學期了。

強尼：求求你盡力把我排進去，不然我要延六個月才能畢業。

01 留學生與外派人員

02 上班族

03 異國情侶

04 背包客和觀光客

 **慣用語**

1. screw up 搞砸了、完蛋了

I have no idea how to fix this assignment. I am totally **screwed up**.

我不知道這份作業還能怎麼更改，我真的完蛋了。

---

2. pull out 取消

I am sorry I have to **pull out** from the tutorial today. I was called in for work at last minute.

很抱歉我必須取消今天的討論課程，我臨時被叫去上班。

---

3. over and over 不斷重複

I can't stand Mr. Fleming. He emphasises the same thing **over and over.**

我真受不了富蘭明先生，他一直重複強調一樣的東西。

---

4. pay attention 注意

Make sure you **pay attention** on the details of enrolment. Everything is now done online.

你要注意註冊的細節，現在所有的東西都要上網操作。

---

5. best bet 最好的方式

The last bus has just left. I think your **best bet** would be to come back tomorrow at 8 am.

最後一班車剛走，我建議你最好的方式就是明天早上八點再來。

6. squeeze in   擠進去

How did you manage to **squeeze in** Prof. Hudson's class?
You are so lucky.

你怎麼有辦法擠進去哈森教授的課？你真的太幸運了。

---

7. put off   延期、暫停

The graduation has been **put off** until Oct. Apparently the
faculty couldn't process the result in time.

畢業典禮被延期到十月了，因為學院來不及審核成績。

---

8. drag on   拖時間

We could have finished the class half an hour ago, but Prof.
Torres just kept **dragging on.**

要不是妥瑞斯教授不斷的拖時間，我們其實半小時前就可以下課。

Unit 4 銀行開戶

前情提要

Belinda 昨天剛到澳洲，帶了一些證明文件現在正在銀行辦理開戶，行員卻對於開戶文件有疑問。

人物角色

- Belinda 留學生
- Mary Ann 銀行行員

情境對話　MP3 04

Belinda: I know what you are saying, but I was told all I need is the letter from the university to prove I am a student which entitles me to open a student account. **I was not aware** I

柏琳達：我知道你的意思，可是有人跟我說我只需要大學出的證明信函說我是學生，這樣我就可以開一個學生帳戶。我不知

also need to bring a proof of address as well.

Mary Ann: Well, because you are an overseas student, we need to verify the documents carefully. Do you have anything which can prove you will be staying in the university dormitory?

Belinda: I only arrived in the country last night. All I have is a receipt to prove I paid for the accommodation for this semester. If this wasn't sufficient, I really don't know what to do. Would you consider calling the university to verify my address? Tell me what else I can do.

道我還需要地址證明。

瑪麗安：嗯，因為你是國際學生，所以我們需要小心地審核所有文件，你可以提出你住在學校宿舍的證明嗎？

柏琳達：我昨天才抵達，我只有一張宿舍繳費的收據，證明繳了一學期。如果這樣無法接受的話，那我不知道要怎麼辦。或是你可以直接打電話給我的學校，跟他們確認我的地址，這是我唯一想到的辦法。

01 留學生與外派人員

02 上班族

03 異國情侶

04 背包客和觀光客

慣用語

1. **I know what you are saying** 我知道你想說什麼

I know what you are saying, but I already have my mind made up.

我知道你想說什麼，可是我已經決定了要這麼做。

---

2. **be aware of** 小心

Make sure you read through the contract before you sign it. Be particularly aware of those terms and conditions.

在你簽約之前，記得要仔細看過合約。尤其是那些註記。

---

3. **dead-end** 困住了，沒有辦法了，死路一條

We got to try something else, this is a **dead-end.**

我們要想其他辦法，這個方法不行。

---

4. **make sure** 要記得

Please **make sure** to call the customer service next week to activate your key card.

下星期請記得打電話到客服中心開你的金融卡。

---

5. **what are the catches?** 有什麼沒有告訴我的

This student account sounds amazing, but **what are the catches?**

這個學生帳戶聽起來很棒，可是有沒有什麼我應該知道的？

6. **private and confidential**　私密的

Please keep your bank statements at a safe place, they are **private and confidential**.

請把你的銀行對帳單保管好，那些都是很私密的文件。

----

7. **being upfront**　醜話說在前頭、開誠布公的

I wish the bank **could be** more **upfront** about the credit card charges. I was shocked to see how much interest they charged.

我情願銀行能開誠布公的解釋信用卡的費用，我看到他們收的利息費用嚇了一大跳。

----

8. **I can live with that**　我可以接受

The e-statement would be ok for me. **I can live with that**.

E 化帳單就可以，我可以接受。

Unit 5 作業要求 延期交件

前情提要

Jerry 一直以來都半工半讀，可是這學期的課程，作業的交期都剛好在同一週，他想去問問看教授是不是可以讓他延遲一個星期交。

人物角色

- Jerry 留學生
- Professor Williamson 威廉森教授

情境對話 `MP3 05`

Jerry: I know you don't like to hear about this, but I am here to ask for the deferral for the final assignment. All I am asking is just one extra week.

傑瑞：我知道你聽到這個一定不高興，但是我不得已要來跟您要求期末作業需要延期交件，只要給我多一個星期就好。

Professor Williamson: Reason be-ing?

威廉森教授：是什麼原因？

Jerry: My parents **made it clear** that I have to be able to support myself **even if** I am a full time student. I **work my ass off** juggling between two part-time jobs and a full time study. You got to **give me some credit for it**.

傑瑞：我爸媽明確的要求我一定要自力更生，就算我是全職的學生也是一樣。我很努力地兼了兩份差還要當全職的學生，這樣應該算是正當理由吧！

Professor Williamson: That's not my problem. You should have planned it better.

威廉森教授：那不是我的問題，你應該更有效率的安排你的時間。

Jerry: I am enrolled in 3 units this semester and how they schedule the assignments are **out of my hands.** All of the assignments are due in the same week. I just need some extra help.

傑瑞：我這學期選了三門課，我沒有辦法控制老師要怎麼安排作業的時間表，所有的作業都需要在同一個星期交件，我只是需要多一點幫助。

01 留學生與外派人員

02 上班族

03 異國情侶

04 背包客和觀光客

 慣用語

1. make it clear 清楚，明確

I am not quite sure whether I got you, could you **make it clear**?

我沒聽懂你想說什麼，可以說的明確一點嗎？

---

2. even if 甚至，就算是

I have to finish the assignment tonight **even if** the house caught on fire.

就算房子燒起來，我今天晚上也一定要把這份作業寫完。

---

3. work my ass off 努力付出

I worked our ass off for this assignment. I can't believe we only got a B+.

我為了這個作業這麼認真，我真不敢相信我們只拿到 B+。

---

4. juggle between 蠟燭兩頭燒、兩方面

I am **juggling between** work and study. I have no time to sleep.

我又要工作又要讀書，我連睡覺的時間都沒有。

---

5. give me some credit for it 給我一點認同

I am trying so hard to get this right, you got to **give me some credit for it**.

我很認真地想把事情做好，你也多少給我一點認同。

6. out of someone's hands   不在某人的掌握之中

How do I know he wouldn't do his part, this is **out of my hands**.

我怎麼知道他會不做他負責的部分，這我真的無法控制。

---

7. make an effort   做出努力、表示認真

I know my assignment was not perfect, but I did **made an effort**.

我知道我的作業不是很完美，可是我真的有努力。

---

8. stand on someone's own feet   自力更生

I am trying to prove to my parents I don't need their help. I can **stand on my own feet**.

我試著要向我父母證明我可以自力更生，不需要他們的幫助。

Unit 6 科目被當 見教授

📋 前情提要

學校成績公布之後 Zoe 發現她經濟學只差兩分被當掉了，要重修。她決定去問教授是不是可以重新校閱她的成績

👤 人物角色

● Zoe 留學生
● Professor Hopkins 霍普金斯教授

👄 情境對話　　　MP3 06

Zoe: Hi, Professor Hopkins, I am here to **have a chat** about my result.

若儀：您好，霍普金斯教授，我想來跟您談談我的成績。

Professor Hopkins: Let me **bring up** your record. Well, you are **two**

霍普金斯教授：讓我調你的資料出來看一下。嗯，

marks short for passing which is a shame.

Zoe: I wondered whether it is possible for me to redo my mid-term paper see if I can make up for those two marks that I need. You can check my attendance, I never missed a single lecture, and I got **30 out of 40** in my final.

Professor Hopkins: Well, considering you did quite well in your final exam. I would **go out of my way** to help you. I will give you a week. Come and see me next Wednesday and I will **go through** your paper again.

你其實差兩分就可及格，真可惜。

若儀：我想問問看是不是可以讓我重做我的期中作業，看看我是不是可以多得到我需要的兩分，你可以查查看我的出席率，我從來沒有缺課，我的期末考也有 **75** 分。

霍普金斯教授：這麼說來你的期末考還考得不錯，我特別幫你一個忙，給你一個禮拜，下星期三帶作業來給我看看。

慣用語

1. **have a chat** 聊聊

Can I **have a chat** with you about how to prepare for the final exam please?

我可以跟您談談如何準備期末考嗎？

---

2. **bring up** 調閱

Can you **bring up** the record to see whether I have any outstanding books please?

可以麻煩你調出我的資料看看我是不是有書還沒還？謝謝。

---

3. **short for passing** 差…就及格

I should have worked harder. I am only a few marks **short for passing** the subject.

早知道我應該認真一點，我只差幾分就可以及格了。

---

4. **30 out of 40 (30/40)** 七十五分

The assignments worth 60 percent and I got 40 out of 60, plus the **30 out of 40** from the final exam. I passed the subject with 70 out of 100 in total.

作業的比重是 60 分，其中我拿到了 40 分。再加上期末考的 40 分裡我拿到了 30 分。我以 70 的總分修完這門課。

---

5. **go out of someone's way** 特別

I realised he **went out of his way** to make the meeting today.

He had to change his shift from the morning to the afternoon.

我現在才知道他為了今天的會議,特別把早班調成下午班。

---

6. go through　經歷

I don't want to **go through** this again. Please let me pass this subject.

我真的不想再重新經歷一次,求求你讓我及格。

---

7. look into　查證

Leave this with me if you don't have time, I will **look into** it.

如果你沒有時間就把這個交給我,我來查查看。

---

8. make it happen　執行

Not to worry, I will **make it happen.**

別擔心,我會處理。

Unit 7 買學生票沒帶證件

 前情提要

　　Julia 跟同學要去看電影，排到她時才發現她沒帶學生證不能買學生票。她的包包裡剛好有一份學校的作業，她想說服售票員賣學生票給她。

 人物角色

- ◉ Julia 留學生
- ◉ Kimberly 售票員

情境對話 `MP3 07`

Julia: Oh no! I just realized I left my student ID in the dorm. Can I still get a student ticket?

茱莉亞：喔糟糕！我剛剛才發現我的學生證丟在宿舍裡。我還可以買學生票嗎？

Kimberly: I am sorry. I have to verify

金柏莉：很抱歉我必須看

the ID before I can sell you the student ticket.

過你的證件才可以賣學生票給你。

Julia: I know I should have my student ID to be able to entitle student discount. Let me see what else I got. I actually have a copy of my assignment, and it is dated last week. I think it should be good enough to prove I am currently enrolled. Come on, I know you can **make the final call.**

茉莉亞：我知道我必須要有學生證才可以享有學生折扣，讓我看看我還有什麼，我剛好有一份作業，上面的日期是上星期。這應該足以證明我是在學學生了吧！別這樣嘛，我知道你有權力決定。

Kimberly: Well, I supposed I can **look the other way**. **That's good enough for me**.

金柏莉：嗯，我看我就網開一面好了，這樣就足以證明了。

Julia: Thanks heaps! You are the best! I am sure no one **goes this far** to **scam the system.**

茉莉亞：太感謝你了，你真是個好人！ 我知道應該沒有人會為了騙一張學生票而做到這種程度的吧！

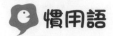 慣用語

1. make the final call　有權力決定

You'd better check with the manager because he **makes the final call.**

你最好跟經理確認一下，因為他有權力決定。

---

2. look the other way　網開一面

I tried to **look the other way**, but what he did is just unacceptable.

我是想對他網開一面，可是他做出的事實在太不能讓人接受。

---

3. good enough for me　我可以接受

The shirt doesn't need to be fancy. As long as it is my size, **it is good enough for me.**

襯衫不用太搶眼，只要是我能穿的就可以。

---

4. thanks heaps　很感謝

Thanks heaps for picking me up; otherwise, I would be stuck here for hours.

謝謝你來接我，不然我就要在這裡等好幾個小時。

---

5. you are the best　你太棒了

I can't believe you brought me dinner for me, **you are the best!**

真不敢相信你帶晚餐來看我，你真是太好了!

6. **go this far** 做到這種程度

We can't quit right this project right now. We already **went this far.**

我們不能就這樣放棄這個專案，我們已經做到這種程度了。

---

7. **scam the system** 騙錢、騙福利

You do realise **scam the** tax **system** is a crime. You will get caught sooner or later.

你知道騙國稅局是犯罪的行為，你遲早會被抓到的。

---

8. **more bang for the buck** 超值的、比較划算

If you wanted to get **more bang for the buck,** you should go to the movies on student nights which is 50 percent off.

學生之夜去看電影是比較划算的，都是半價。

Memo

37

Unit 8 宿舍室友吵鬧

🧠 前情提要

　　Paul 的室友幾乎天天晚上都帶朋友回來喝酒聊天，吵得他不能睡。他忍無可忍決定跟他抱怨。

👤 人物角色

- Paul 留學生
- Cameron 外籍室友

👄 情境對話　　　　MP3 08

Paul: hey, I know you are probably still hangover, but I really need to speak to you about something. It has been bothering me for a long time.

Cameron: What is it？

保羅：我知道你可能還在宿醉，可是我真的忍無可忍了，一定要跟你說，我已經忍耐很久了。

卡麥倫：到底什麼事？

Paul: I **had enough** of the chatting, and the loud music every night. All I want to do is to **have a good night sleep**, I got work to go to in the morning and classes in the afternoon.

Cameron: I am sorry but you can join us if you want.

Paul: I don't want to join you, and I am not telling you what not to do, but every night of the week is just **too much to handle**. I can tolerateit it on the weekends, but please, not the week nights.

保羅：我真的受不了你每天晚上又是聊天又是吵鬧的音樂，我真的只想睡個好覺，你要知道我早上要上班，下午還要卜課。

卡麥倫：不好意思啦！你也可以加入我們啊！

保羅：我不想加入你們！我也不是教你都不要這樣，只是一個禮拜七天都這樣真的太過分了。如果只是週末我還可以忍受，可是拜託，一到五不要好不好。

01 留學生與外派人員

02 上班族

03 異國情侶

04 背包客和觀光客

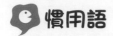 慣用語

1. had enough　受夠了

I am at the boiling point, I **had enough** of his offensive behavior every time he got drunk.

我快要忍不住了，我受夠了他每次喝醉的脫序行為。

---

2. have a good night sleep　好好睡一覺

All I want is to **have a good night sleep**. Is this too much to ask for?

我真的只想好好睡一覺，這樣的要求很過分嗎？

---

3. too much to handle　很難接受

Taking evening shifts is getting to be **too much to handle**. I hardly get any sleep.

我越來越不能接受上晚班，我一天沒睡幾個小時。

---

4. in a roll　連續

Please don't torture me with the Thai food challenge, 5 days **in a roll** is way too much.

請不要用泰國菜挑戰來整我，5 天連續吃實在是受不了。

---

5. a piece of quiet　片刻的寧靜

I can only get **a piece of quiet** when my roommate is out.

我只有在我室友出去的時候才能享受片刻的寧靜。

6. **day in and day out**　每天不斷重複

I can't stand the news channels are always on rerun **day in and day out.**

我受不了新聞台每天不斷重播。

---

7. **party animal**　派對狂

I just hope my next roommate is not a **party animal** like Cameron.

我只希望我下一個室友不要像卡麥倫那樣瘋夜店。

---

8. **get wasted**　喝得爛醉

All he wants to do for his birthday is to **get wasted.** Let's just take him to a night club!

他的生日願望就是想喝個爛醉，我們就帶他去夜店吧！

Unit 9 共用廚房誰整理

前情提要

Tracey 的室友 Stephen 吃完飯總是把碗盤丟在水槽不洗，Tracy 每次要煮飯前都還要先把他的碗盤洗好才有碗盤可以用。這一天室友又在煮飯了，Tracey 決定提醒他。

人物角色

- Tracey 留學生
- Stephen 外籍室友

情境對話 `MP3 09`

Tracey: Hey Stephen, can I ask you to clean up the dishes once you are done cooking? **Just in case you didn't notice.** I have been cleaning

崔西：嘿，史蒂芬，我可以麻煩你在煮完飯之後把碗洗一洗嗎？你可能沒有注意到，這一個禮拜多來

up after you for more than a week now.

都是我在幫你洗碗。

Stephen: Oh.. Did I not do that? Ok..

史蒂芬：喔⋯我真的沒有洗嗎？ 那⋯好⋯

Tracey: I am not trying to be a **pain in the ass,** but I am just **sick of** tidying up for others. I got lots of studies to catch up. I don't mind help you out **once a while**, if you got **caught up with things,** but not all the time.

崔西：我不是想要找你麻煩，可是我真的受不了一直幫人收拾善後。我自己有很多書要讀，如果你忙的話，我不介意偶爾幫一次，可是不能每次都指望我。

Stephen: I am sorry I didn't realise I haven't been doing it. I guess **my mind was somewhere** else.

史蒂芬：真的很抱歉，我一直沒注意到我都沒做，可能我都在想別的事。

Tracey: That's all right, I am not trying to make you feel bad, I just want to **draw your attention.**

崔西：沒關係，我不是想讓你覺得難堪，我只是想讓你注意到這件事。

 慣用語

1. just in case you didn't notice　你可能沒注意到

I have moved your books to the bottom of the shelf **just in case you didn't notice**.

你可能沒注意到，我把你的書搬到櫃子的下面了。

---

2. pain in the ass　找麻煩

My brother is such a **pain in the ass**. He keeps hiding my makeups.

我弟弟真的很煩，他故意把我的化妝品藏起來。

---

3. sick of　受不了

I am **sick of** going to the same job everyday. I think it is time for a change.

我受不了每天都做一樣的工作，是應該要改變一下了。

---

4. once a while　偶爾

I just want to chill out **once a while**, just sit around and do nothing.

我有時候就只想放鬆，坐下來什麼都不做。

---

5. caught up with　為了某事在忙

Sorry I was late, I was **caught up with** the peak hour traffic.

抱歉我遲到了，被塞在尖峰時間的車陣中。

6. my mind was somewhere else　心不在焉

I found it hard to focus this morning. **My mind was somewhere else.**

我今天早上沒有辦法專心，就是心不在焉

---

7. draw your attention　提醒你

Just to **draw your attention**. Your mail is on the kitchen bench top.

想提醒你，你的信件在廚房的餐檯上。

---

8. stand in someone's shoes　站在我的立場

Why don't you **stand in my shoes,** it is hard to live without your parents' support.

為什麼你不站在我的立場想想看，沒有父母的支持不是那麼容易。

Unit 10 房屋修繕

前情提要

Peter 不只一次跟房東講過浴室有漏水的問題，可是房東遲遲沒派人來修，Peter 只好去找房東抗議。

人物角色

● Peter 房客
● Mr. Moore 房東

情境對話　　　MP3 10

Peter: Hello Mr. Moore. I came to see you today because I reported the problem of the leaking tap in my bathroom last month, and you promised me the plumber would be here in a

彼得：摩爾先生您好，我今天來是因為我上個月就跟你說過浴室的水龍頭在漏水。你答應我水電工這幾天就會來，可是一直都

few days, but till now he is **nowhere to be seen** still.

Mr. Moore: Oh... my apology. I will **get onto it** on Monday.

Peter: Do you realize how much we have to pay for our last water bill? It cost extra 50 dollars! I am only a student, and I don't make a lot of money and I hope you are willing to cover the extra cost until the tap is fixed. If the plumber did not **rock up** on Monday, I would hire one to fix it myself and send the bill to you.

沒有人來修。

摩爾先生：不好意思，我星期一會馬上辦。

彼得：你知道我們上個月的水費繳多少錢嗎？比平常多 50 美金。我只是個學生，賺的錢不多，我希望在水龍頭修好之前你要負擔額外的水費。如果水電工星期一再不來修，我只好自己請人來修然後把帳單寄給你。

冤家英語

慣用語

1. **nowhere to be seen** 找不到人

Does anyone know where Elliot is? He should have been here half an hour ago but still **nowhere to be seen.**

有人知道艾利耶在哪裡嗎？他半小時前就應該到了，到現在還是找不到人。

---

2. **get onto it** 會處理

I will **get onto it** right now. I know this is an urgent matter.

我現在馬上處理，我知道這是急事。

---

3. **rock up** 出現

Thank God you just **rock up**. I can really do with your help now.

太棒了你出現的正是時候，我真的很需要你的幫忙。

---

4. **out of pocket** 自己掏腰包

I can't believe that I had to pay USD 150 **out of pocket** for dental check-up. That's ridiculous.

我不敢相信看牙醫還要給美金 150 塊的自付額，真的太扯了。

---

5. **track down** 尋找

I have been trying to **track down** my landlord. He is not answering my calls.

我在找我的房東，可是他一直不接我電話。

6. **good as new** 跟新的一樣、修好了

All it needed is a replacement washer. The tap is now **good as new.**

只需要更換一個墊片，水龍頭就修好了。

---

7. **slip through the cracks** 被忽略了、沒有被處理

I am so sorry, it must have **slipped through the cracks** somehow. I will organise it for you right away.

很抱歉不知道什麼原因沒有被處理，我現在馬上為你安排。

---

8. **straight away** 立即、馬上

Please do it **straight away** with the tasks which labelled "Urgent."

那些標示「急件」的事情，麻煩你馬上處理。

Unit 11 退租押金

前情提要

Claire 是由公司外派到美國的專案經理,一到美國就租了一個兩房的公寓。三年租約期滿公司要把她調回台灣,要退租前房東來檢查房子發現廚房的櫃子被弄壞了,要扣她押金。

人物角色

● Claire 外派人員
● Mrs. Ferguson 房東太太

情境對話　　MP3 11

Mrs. Ferguson: I am happy with the general condition of wall and the carpet, but the kitchen cabinet doors need to be replaced. The condition is appalling. I would have to deduct

佛格森太太:這房子的牆面及地毯大概的情況都還好,可是廚房儲物櫃的門需要更換,怎麼會弄得這麼糟?我必須扣你 150

USD 150 from your bond.

Claire: I do apologize, my boyfriend thought the door was jammed and he pulled it too hard. The hinges just came off. I think you can easily repair it if you get a handyman in. It would not cost USD 150, would it? I think USD 100 would be a fair price. I mean the condition of the cabinet door was not too flash when we moved in **to start with**. You can **see for yourself** we do try to **take a good care** of this place.

美金的押金。

克萊兒：真的很抱歉，我男朋友以為櫥櫃門卡住了就用力拉，誰知道太用力了，櫃子的樞軸就掉下來了。我覺得如果找個雜工來處理應該很容易更換，這應該不需要 150 美金吧！100 應該就可以了吧！因為我們搬進來的時候櫥櫃門本來就有點舊，你應該也看的出來我們一直都很照顧這個房子。

01 留學生與外派人員
02 上班族
03 異國情侶
04 背包客和觀光客

 慣用語 ---------------

1. **to start with** 首先，一開始

I would like to introduce myself **to start with.**

首先我想先介紹我自己

---

2. **see for yourself** 你自己看看

I don't have to try hard to convince you, you can **see for yourself.**

我不用努力地說服你，你可以自己用眼睛看看。

---

3. **take a good care** 很用心照顧

I hope you will feel better soon, please **take a good care** of yourself.

我希望你會很快康復，請好好照顧自己。

---

4. **normal wear and tear** 正常磨損

A burn mark on the carpet is not **normal wear and tear.**

地毯上燒過的痕跡是不屬於正常磨損的。

---

5. **take it easy** 放輕鬆

Please **take it easy**, a rental inspection is not as bad.

放輕鬆，房東來檢查房子並沒有那麼糟糕。

---

6. **break the lease** 未期滿退租

I got transferred to a different branch in New York. Unfortunately, I have to **break the lease** in a month time.

我被調到紐約的一個分公司，不好意思我下個月要提早退租。

---

7. **make up the differences**　補差額

I understand I would have to **make up the difference** for 3 month rent.

我知道我還要補你三個月的房租。

---

8. **end on good terms**　好好地結束、保持關係良好

I really wish we could **end on good terms** because you have been nice to us after we moved in.

我希望這不會影響我們的好關係，因為我們搬進來之後你一直都很照顧我們。

Memo

Unit 12 安裝電話費用的紛爭

🌀 前情提要

　　Andy 搬進新租的房子要請電話公司來安裝家用電話，在比較幾家公司之後他決定跟 CCphone 簽約，可是安裝之後卻收到帳單說需要付安裝費用，之前業務員説是沒有安裝費用的，Andy 回到店裡面去找那個業務員。

👤 人物角色

　⦿ Andy 新電話用戶
　⦿ Mark 業務員

👄 情境對話　　　　　　MP3 12

Mark: How is your home phone going?

馬克：你的家用電話都裝好了嗎？

Andy: It is going ok, but I received

安迪：還好，可是我收到

the bill asking for the installation fee, and I remembered clearly there is no installation fee.

Mark: There is no installation fee, if you are switching from other phone company, but for the new client there is an installation charge.

Andy: Well, that is not what I was told. I would not have **signed up** with you if I knew, there is going to be installation charge. What form do I have to sign to cancel the service?

Mark: I am sorry you are **under the wrong impression**, let me check with my boss and see what I can do.

Andy: **Now you are talking**, I am sure you don't want to lose a customer.

一張帳單說要收安裝費，我記得很清楚你說過沒有安裝費的。

馬克：如果你有安裝過別家公司的電話，那是沒有安裝費的。可是如果是全新用戶那就會有。

安迪：可是我聽到的不是這樣，我如果知道有安裝費用我就不會選擇你們公司。那我要取消，要填什麼表格呢？

馬克：不好意思你可能誤會我的意思，讓我問一下我的上司看能怎麼處理。

安迪：這才對，你一定也不想失去一個客戶。

 **慣用語**

1. sign up　簽約

Is it possible to **sign up** for only 6 months? I can't do one year contract.

可以只簽 6 個月的約嗎？我沒有辦法簽一年。

---

2. under the wrong impression　聽錯了、想錯了

I was **under the wrong impression.** I thought he said he was single, isn't he?

我一直想錯了，我以為他說他還單身，不是嗎？

---

3. now you talking!　這樣才對嘛

Now you talking! I think this could work.

這樣才對嘛！ 這樣我就覺得可行了。

---

4. that's bull　亂講、不可能 (= that's bullshit)

What do you mean that I can't pull out half way? **That's bull.**

為什麼我不能半途退出？不可能。

---

5. deal with it　硬著頭皮處理

I can't stand Mrs. Powell, but she always asks for me personally. Guess I just have to **deal with it.**

我很受不了包爾太太，可是她每次都指名找我，我也只好硬著頭皮去了。

6. **never hear the end of it**　抱怨連連

I'd better sort this out for Erica; otherwise, I would **never hear the end of it** from her.

我最好幫艾瑞卡把事情處理好，不然她會一直不停地抱怨。

---

7. **forget about it**　算了

Forget about it, I really don't think this is for me.

算了不要再説了，我真的覺得這不適合我。

Unit 13 買車

🧠 前情提要

Jeffery 買了一台二手車,回來之後卻發現有問題,拿去另一間車廠估價後說要花 USD 5000 換引擎。他回去跟車廠的業務爭論。

👤 人物角色

- Carter 客戶
- Russell 車廠業務員

👄 情境對話 ⸻⸻ MP3 13

Carter: Hey, you sold me **a piece of crap**! The car broke down on the side of the road 3 days after I took it home. I had it checked out by the other car yard. They quoted me USD 5000 for

卡特:嘿!你賣了一台爛車給我!那台車才牽回家三天就在路邊熄火,我拿到別家車廠去檢查,他們說要花 5000 塊修理,

repair. Apparently, the engine is totally **wore out.**

Russell: Well, what do you expect when you buy a used car, you got to be prepared and understand there would be some problems need to **be sorted out further down the track.**

Carter: I understand but USD 3000 should get you a **half decent** car. You know paying USD 3000 for the car and USD 5000 to get the engine replaced is just ridiculous. If I knew this early, I would not touch this car. You can take the car, I just want my money back.

引擎早就壞掉了！

羅素：嗯，你買的是二手車還想怎麼樣，你應該有心理準備遲早會有一些問題。

卡特：我懂，可是三千塊應該可以買到還可以的車。你說花了三千元買車再花五千元換引擎是不是很蠢。早知道是這樣我才不會碰這台車。你把車拿回去，我只要把錢拿回來就好。

 慣用語

1. piece of crap　爛貨、品質很差

I spent USD 500 buying a used fridge, but it turned out to be **a piece of crap.**

我花了 500 美金買了一台二手冰箱，可是卻是一台爛貨。

---

2. wore out　嚴重磨損、快壞了

The front tyres of my car are pretty much **wore out**. They need to be replaced.

我車的前輪差不多要磨壞了，需要更換。

---

3. sort out　處理

Just leave the car here with us, we will **sort it out** for you.

請把車留下來，我們幫你處理。

---

4. further down the track　再過一陣子、之後

If you buy second hand items, you got to expect there might be problems **further down the track.**

如果你買二手貨，應該要有心理準備過一陣子都會有問題。

---

5. half decent　品質尚可

My budge is limited, but I am looking for a **half decent** car.

我的預算有限，可是我想找一台還可以的車。

---

6. get rid of it　丟掉，處理掉

I really don't want to see this ugly dress again, please **get rid**

of it for me.

我真的不想再看到這件醜洋裝，請幫我把它丟掉。

---

7. ripping someone off blind　存心騙某人錢

Don't believe anything he said, I think that sales is **ripping me off blind.**

千萬別相信他，我覺得他是存心騙我錢。

---

8. piss off　氣死了

Talking to someone like that is **pissing me off.**

跟這種人說話真是氣死我了。

Memo

Unit 14 車窗被砸

🗨️ 前情提要

Danny 的車停在住家附近的路邊，早上出門時發現車窗被砸破，他懷疑是其中一個鄰居，因為他們常為了停車的問題爭吵。

👤 人物角色

- Danny 車主
- Roy 鄰居

👄 情境對話 ⸺ MP3 14

Danny: I knew that was you, I saw you walking up and down the street after I parked the car.

丹尼：我知道是你幹的！我停好車之後有看到你在街上閒逛。

Roy: It wasn't me! I didn't do it. How dare you **accuse me for** something

羅伊：真的不是我，我沒有做！你怎麼可以誣賴我

like that, I do have a problem with you but I am not that nasty.

Danny: Why were you being sneaky then?

Roy: What sneaky! I was just taking a walk, **what's that got to do with** you?

Danny: Cut the crap! I don't believe anything comes out of your mouth. You think I got no proof, let me call the police and pull out the footage of the surveillance camera. Let's see what else you got to say. Just let me tell you, if you were caught doing it, you'd better **watch your ass**.

會做這樣的事。我是跟你有過節可是我沒有這麼惡劣。

丹尼：那你為什麼鬼鬼祟祟的？

羅伊：我哪有鬼鬼祟祟！我只是在散步，這干你什麼事？

丹尼：少來！我才不相信你講的話。你以為我沒有證據，等我叫警察來調出監視器的畫面，到時候看你有什麼好說。我跟你說，如果真的抓到是你做，你就給我小心一點！

 慣用語

1. accuse for　誣賴

Stop **accusing** me **for** things I didn't do.

我沒做的事請不要誣賴我。

---

2. what's that got to do with you　干你什麼事

Yes, I like to wear tight dresses, **what's that got to do with you?**

是的，我喜歡穿緊身裙，這干你什麼事？

---

3. cut the crap　別再廢話了

Just **cut the crap,** I know you really want me to turn off that music.

別再廢話了，我知道你只是要我把音樂關掉。

---

4. watch your ass　小心一點

You'd better **watch your ass.** Don't let me see you again!

你最好小心一點，別再讓我遇到你。

---

5. don't be a tool　別像個白癡一樣

Hey, get real! **Don't be a tool.**

嘿!別鬧了，不要像個白癡一樣。

---

6. what the hell is this　這是搞什麼

What the hell is this! Look at what she is wearing.

這是搞什麼！你看她穿的是什麼鬼樣子。

---

7. **teach someone a lesson　你會學到教訓的**

A speeding ticket is just to **teach you a lesson** so you don't do it again.

超速罰單是要教訓你，這樣你以後才不會再犯。

---

8. **it sucks　真糟糕，很爛，很不爽**

It sucks to see my car window smashed first thing in the morning.

一早起來就看到車窗被砸，心裡真的很不爽

Memo

Unit 15 預約看醫生

前情提要

　　Tony 覺得很不舒服，想去看醫生可是打電話過去今天都約滿了。他想請護士幫個忙是不是能讓他候補。

人物角色

● Tony 病人
● Chelsea 護士雀兒喜

情境對話

MP3 15

Tony: Hello, I am calling to check whether there is a vacancy for Dr. Howard to see me this morning. **I am not feeling 100 %.**

湯尼：您好，我想問一下能不能掛哈沃醫生今天早上的門診？我覺得非常不舒服。

Nurse Chelsea: Hang on a second,

護士雀兒喜：請等一下，

I will check his availability. Well, I am sorry he is **fully booked** today.

我查一下預約紀錄。嗯，不好意思他今天都約滿了。

Tony: What about other doctors? Maybe Dr. Abbott?

湯尼：那其他醫生呢？查一下亞伯特醫生好嗎？

Nurse Chelsea: He is also fully booked unfortunately.

護士雀兒喜：很可惜他也約滿了。

Tony: Can I ask for a huge favour please? I know you don't normally do this, but would you please take my contact details and call me back if **any of the vacancies come up?** I would be home all day. Any time is a good time as long as I can get to see a doctor today. I live very close, I can be there within 10 mins.

湯尼：我可以請您幫個大忙嗎？我知道你們通常不會這樣做，可是您是不是可以留下我的聯絡方式，如果有人取消請通知我好嗎？我整天都會在家，所以什麼時間都可以，只要看的到醫生就好。我住得很近，十分鐘就能到。

01 留學生與外派人員

02 上班族

03 異國情侶

04 背包客和觀光客

💬 慣用語

1. not feeling 100 percent 覺得不舒服

Can we change the meeting to tomorrow please? I am just **not feeling 100 percent.**

會議可以改明天嗎？我實在不太舒服。

---

2. fully booked 約滿了

We have to go to a different clinic if you wanted to see the doctor today, they are **fully booked** here.

如果你今天一定要看到醫生的話，那我們要到別家醫院，因為都預約滿了。

---

3. can I ask for a favor 可以幫我個忙嗎？

Can I ask for a favor please? I feel terrible, can you take me to the hospital please?

可以幫我個忙嗎？我很不舒服，可以帶我去醫院嗎？

---

4. come up 出現

This kind of opportunity does not **come up** all the time. You'd better grab it.

這種機會不是常常出現，你要把握。

---

5. work around it 可以配合

Any time is a good time, I can **work around it**.

什麼時候都可以，我隨時可以配合。

6. jump the queue　插隊

It will be unfair if I let you **jump the queue**.

如果我讓你插隊的話，那對別人很不公平。

---

7. work your magic　想想辦法

Please **work your magic,** it will be great if I can get an appointment this morning.

求求你幫我想想辦法，如果今天早上可以排進去的話就太好了。

---

8. pass out　昏倒，暈倒

I think I really need to go to hospital now. I feel like I am about to **pass out.**

我覺得我真的應該去醫院了，我好像快昏倒了。

Unit 16 有人插隊

前情提要

Campbell 在超市買東西，前面有人的推車剛好擋在路中間。那個人又一直在看同一樣東西，無法決定。Campbell 等得很不耐煩，就出聲兇她。

人物角色

- *Campbell* 被推車擋到的人
- *Carrie* 在購物的人

情境對話　MP3 16

Campbell: Hey, <u>**are you done yet?**</u> Just pick one and <u>**move out of the way**</u>, I am trying to get through here.

坎伯：嘿！你有完沒完，隨便選一個然後趕快讓開，我要過去。

Carrie: Excuse me, <u>**mind your lan-**</u>

凱莉：什麼！你講話好聽

guage! I am sorry my trolley **got in your way,** I will move it for you, but you don't have to be so rude. I am just doing my shopping here.

Campbell: I am sorry if I **come across** as rude. **I am just not myself** today. Things **are not exactly going my way** today, now I made it worse. My apology

Carrie: Apology accepted. **I feel for you,** but it is not my fault. Now I am having a bad day because I got yelled at by a complete stranger.

一點好嘛！很抱歉我推車擋到你的路，我會讓路給你可是你也不用這麼沒禮貌，我也只不過是來買東西。

坎伯：對不起如果你覺得我是個很無理的人，我今天不知道是怎麼回事，做什麼事都不順利，現在更糟了，請接受我的道歉。

凱莉：沒關係。我很同情你，可是你不順並不是我的錯，我無端端被一個不認識的人罵，那不是換我倒楣嗎？

慣用語

1. are you done?　做完了嗎？

Are you done with your meal? Can I clear the table now?

你吃完了嗎？我可以收桌子了沒？

---

2. move out of the way　讓開

I will **move out of your way**. You seem busy here.

我還是不要妨礙你好了，你好像很忙。

---

3. mind your language　說話好聽一點

Mind your language, a lady does not speak like that.

說話好聽一點喔，女士不會這樣說話。

---

4. get in your way　擋到你

This kitchen is too small. I always **get in your way** with both of us here.

這個廚房太小了，如果我們兩個同時在裡面的話，我會一直擋到你的路。

---

5. come across　遇見，意外發現

I **came across** this old photo of your dad, while I was sorting out our stuff in the storage.

我在整理儲藏室的東西時意外發現這張你爸爸的舊照片。

---

6. just not myself　不知道怎麼搞的，失魂落魄

I think the work pressure has gotten too much to handle, I am

just not myself lately.

可能工作壓力太大，我最近真不知道怎麼了。

---

7. **things are not going my way**　**諸事不順，很倒楣**

I can't believe someone stole my credit card after I got fried from work. Things **are not going my way** at all. 我真不敢相信我被炒魷魚之後，信用卡還被偷，真的是諸事不順。

---

8. **I feel for you**　**我同情你**

I really feel for you, but I am not sure how I can help you.

我真的很同情你，可是我不知道怎麼幫你。

Memo

01 留學生與外派人員

02 上班族

03 異國情侶

04 背包客和觀光客

Unit
17 申請表填錯

**前情提要**

  Christine 因為工作的需要來報考雅思文能力認證考試，可是線上申請時填錯了組別應該選擇 General 卻誤填為 Academic，一直到考試當天她才發現，她想要試試看是不是可以換組別。

人物角色

- Christine 考生
- Sonya 考場工作人員

情境對話   MP3 17

Christine: I am sorry I just realized I make a mistake on the application. I **meant to** take General training, but I accidently picked Academic. Is it possible for me to change now?

克莉絲汀：不好意思我剛才發現我的申請表填錯了，我應該要選一般訓練組，可是我誤選了學術組。請問可以更換嗎？

Sonya: Well, you should have been more careful, while you are **filling it out**.

Christine: I am really sorry, but I really do need to take General training, because there is **no hope in hell** I would pass Academic.

Sonya: I would suggest you check in as is and if we have any cancellation from General training, we can **swap you over**. Often we do have a few no-shows, but **there is no guarantee**.

Christine: Well, thanks for the advice. I think I would **go ahead** and get checked in for now, but please **keep it in mind** that I need a swap. That will be much appreciated.

桑雅：嗯，你填表的時候應該小心一點。

克莉絲汀：我真的很抱歉，可是我真的需要考一般訓練組，因為我絕對不可能通過學術組的考試。

桑雅：我會建議你先以學術組的身分入場，如果有一般訓練組的考生沒來，我們再把你換過去。通常都會有人缺考，但這無法保證。

克莉絲丁：嗯，謝謝你的建議，我就照這樣先入場，再麻煩你記得我需要更換。真的很感謝你。

 **慣用語**

1. meant to　原本要，應該要

I **meant to** go to down town city, but I took the exit and ended up in Soho.

我是想要到市中心的，可是我下錯交流道跑到蘇活區了。

---

2. fill out　填寫

There are so many forms needed to be **filled out** when you are applying for the scholarship.

要申請獎學金需要填的表格很多。

---

3. no hope in hell　不可能

There is **no hope in hell** he can make it to the test in time if he didn't drive.

如果他不開車的話，他是不可能及時趕來考試的。

---

4. swap something/ someone over　換過去，更換

Since you prefer the red one, why don't we **swap over**?

既然你比較喜歡紅色的，為什麼我們不乾脆換過來？

---

5. there is no guaranty　不保證

There is a chance they will take me on board for this project, but **there is no guaranty.**

他們有可能請我來做這個專案，可是還不一定。

6. **go ahead**　照這樣進行

I don't think we can **go ahead** with this without Richard's approval.

在李察同意之前，我們沒有辦法開始。

---

7. **keep it in mind**　記得

Please **keep it in mind** the test starts at 10am Monday morning.

請記得星期一早上十點開始考試。

---

8. **turn out**　結果，變成

It **turns out** I was the first to be tested. I didn't not expect that at all.

結果我是第一個應考的考生，我真的完全沒想到會這樣。

Unit 18 上網購物收到錯誤的商品

 前情提要

Alison 收到與自己訂貨尺寸不符的鞋子，於是致電給客服。

 人物角色

- Alison 客戶
- Tim 客服人員

情境對話 ⸺⸺ MP3 18

Alison: Hi, I ordered a pair of shoes, but what I received is the wrong size.

艾利森：您好，我有訂購一雙鞋，可是我收到的尺寸是錯的。

Timothy: Sure I can organise an exchange for you. What size are you after?

提摩西：好的，我立刻幫您換貨，請問您要哪一個尺寸？

Alison: Perhaps I didn't <u>**make my-self clear.**</u> <u>**What I was trying to say**</u> is, there is a <u>**mix up**</u>, I ordered a size 24 and on the documentation also stated sizc 24, but I actually received size 22 instead. My order number is #332448.

Timothy: Right, sorry for the inconvenience caused. If you can organize the item and the paperwork to be sent back to us, we will organize the exchange for you.

Alison: Do I have to pay for the post-age?

Timothy: Yes, that's correct, but you will not be charged again the postage for us to send the right one for you.

Alison: I don't think it is fair, because it was negligence on your side Why am I <u>**liable for**</u> the return postage? That's a scam.

艾利森：我可能沒有說清楚，我是想說，我訂的是 24 號，文件上也是 24 號，可是實際上我收到的是 22 號。我的訂單號碼是：332448。

提摩西：好的，對您造成的不便很抱歉，如果你可以連鞋子還有文件　起寄回來的話，我們會幫您換貨。

艾利森：那我要付郵資嗎？

提摩西：是的，可是你不需要付我們寄回去的郵資。

艾利森：這不公平吧！因為這是你們的疏忽為什麼我要付寄回去的郵資？這是搶人吧！

慣用語

1. make oneself clear 講清楚

I don't think that he **made himself clear,** I thought he wanted us to wait for further notice.

我覺得他沒有講清楚，我以為他要我們繼續等消息。

---

2. what I try to say 我想說的是

Sorry to confuse you, **what I was trying to say** is, you get 50% off the second pair of shoe you purchased. Not for both pairs.

抱歉沒讓你搞清楚，我想說的是只有第二雙有半價的折扣，不是兩雙都有。

---

3. mix up 搞錯

The courier company **mixed up** the shipments, Mrs. Watkins actually received the order for Mr. Piggott.

快遞公司搞錯了，沃金斯太太收到的是品高先生的訂單。

---

4. liable for 負責

It is possible to change the design, but who is **liable for** the cost?

要改設計可以，可是錢誰要付？

---

5. carrying on 不停的抱怨

Stop **carrying on** like that. No one is going to be happy.

不要這樣不停地抱怨，大家都會不高興。

6. **free of charge** 免費

If you order more than one item today, you will get a crystal wine glass **free of charge** as our gift for you.

如果你今天訂購一個以上的產品，我們會免費送你一個水晶酒杯。

7. **loss for words** 驚訝地說不出話

I could not believe they refuse to exchange it for me. I was **loss for words.**

我不敢相信他們拒絕幫我換貨，我真的不知道要說什麼。

8. **work something out** 想辦法，處理

We can't refund the money, but we will **work something out** for you.

我們沒有辦法退錢給你，可是我們會想辦法幫你處理。

篇章回顧

精選慣用語

1. an arm and a leg 很貴

A decent diamond ring could cost you **an arm and a leg**.

---

2. One click away 只要上網處理

Why don't you register as one of our online banking customer? You can handle all the transactions with only **one click away**.

為什麼不註冊成為我們的網路銀行會員呢？所有的交易都可以上網處理。

---

3. drag on 拖時間

We could have finish the class half an hour ago but Prof. Torres just keep **dragging on.**

要不是妥瑞斯教授不斷的拖時間，我們其實半小時前就可以下課。

4. what are the catches? 有什麼沒有告訴我的

This student account sounds amazing, but_**what are the**

catches?

這個學生帳戶聽起來很棒，可是有沒有什麼我應該知道的？

---

5. **work my ass off** 努力付出

I worked our ass off for this assignment. I can't believe we only got a B+.

我為了這個作業這麼認真，我真不敢相信我們只拿到 B+。

---

6. **more bang for the buck** 超值的、比較划算

If you wanted to get **more bang for the buck,** you should go to the movies on student nights which is 50 percent off.

學生之夜去看電影是比較划算的，都是半價。

---

7. **pain in the ass** 找麻煩

My brother is such a **pain in the ass**, he keeps hiding my makeups.

我弟弟真的很煩，他故意把我的化妝品藏起來。

---

8. **not feeling 100 percent** 覺得不舒服

Can we change the meeting to tomorrow please, I am just **not feeling 100 percent.**

會議可以改明天嗎？我實在不太舒服。

PART 02

上班族

學習進度表

☐ 19. 客戶抱怨   ☐ 28. 上班遲到

☐ 20. 三心二意的客戶 ☐ 29. 忘記上司交代的事

☐ 21. 不守信用   ☐ 30. 效率不佳

☐ 22. 難纏的客戶   ☐ 31. 想加薪

☐ 23. 留言請回電   ☐ 32. 沒有得到想要的職缺

☐ 24. 背後捅人的同事 ☐ 33. 被迫加班

☐ 25. 不做事的同事   ☐ 34. 想換工作

☐ 26. 說錯話   ☐ 35. 其他公司來挖角

☐ 27. 上司不採納你的意見 ☐ 36. 討論不想做的事

看完的單元也別忘了打勾喔！！

Unit 19 客戶抱怨

 前情提要

客戶打電話來抱怨公司出錯貨卻要客戶自行負擔退貨的郵資，Tim 需要跟經理 Richard 確認這該怎麼處理。

人物角色

- Tim 客服人員
- Richard 經理
- Doug 倉儲人員

情境對話　　MP3 19

Tim: Hey Richard, there is a customer on the line **carrying on** about the postage. She is demanding us to refund the postage.

提姆：理查，現在有一個客戶在線上抱怨要付換貨的郵資，他要求我們要退還郵資給她。

Richard: Well, you **know** the company policy **better than I do.** The customers are liable for postage if they wish to exchange.

Tim: This is **a tricky one**, the store man shipped out the wrong item, but on the paperwork she received what she ordered. So I think I'd better check with you.

Richard: Let me guess, Doug was **responsible for** that order?

Tim: You are right. He was **on duty** when the order came in.

Richard: This is the 5th time this month. I think I need to **have a word** with him about this. Just tell the customer **the best we can do** is to give her store credit for it.

查理：嗯，你對公司的退貨制度應該比我還熟，如果要換貨就要自付郵資啊！

提姆：這個情況比較難處理一點。客戶的單據上面是她要的沒錯，可是我們的倉儲人員出錯貨了。所以我才想跟你確認一下要怎麼處理。

理查：讓我猜猜看，是不是道格負責的訂單？

提姆：你猜對了，訂單進來的時候是他值班的沒錯。

理查：這已經是他這個月第五次出錯了，我真的要跟他好好談談。跟客戶說我們最多就只能給她公司的消費禮券。

01 留學生與外派人員

02 上班族

03 異國情侶

04 背包客和觀光客

 慣用語

1. **carry on** 抱怨

Sarah is **carrying on** again about how they refused to refund her the down payment.

莎拉又在抱怨他們怎樣拒絕退回訂金給她。

---

2. **Know something better than someone do/does**
對於某件事比某人還要熟悉

Why are you asking me about taking leaves? You **know the rules better than I do**.

為什麼你一直問我請假的事？你對請假的規定比我還熟。

---

3. **a tricky one** 棘手、不好處理的情況

I am not sure whether to go ahead with rejecting the customer's request, this is **a tricky one.**

我不確定是不是要直接拒絕客戶的要求，因為這是個棘手的情況。

---

4. **be responsible for** 負責

You **are responsible for** taking all the incoming calls.

你的責任就是接電話。

---

5. **on duty** 值班

Who will to be **on duty** this weekend?

這個週末誰值班？

6. have a word　談談

I need to **have a word** with you regarding the latest company policy.

我需要跟你談談最新的公司規定

---

7. the best someone can do　最多，最好就是這樣了

This is the best I can do. I can't offer you anything more.

我沒辦法再多給你了，最多就是這樣了。

---

8. refund policy　退款制度

Can you talk me through your **refund policy** please?

你可以跟我解釋一下你們的退款制度嗎？

Memo

Unit 20 三心二意的客戶

🧠 前情提要

Gary 是公司代表與客戶 Thomas Benson 洽談這個案子好一陣子，前天已經定案了，今天卻又說要改設計。

👤 人物角色

- Gary 公司代表
- Thomas Benson 客戶代表

👄 情境對話　　MP3 20

Thomas: Hello, Gary. Hmm. I know we have finalized the specification **the other day**, but we need some minor adjustments done.

Gary: Oh...Thomas, please don't tell

湯瑪士：你好蓋瑞，嗯，我知道我們那天已經講好規格了，可是我們需要做一些細部的調整。

蓋瑞：天啊！湯瑪士，拜

me that. The paperwork has been done and part of it is already in the production. This doesn't even consider as the **last minute** change.

Thomas: come on Gary, It is **not a big deal**, just some minor changes. It is in the later production stage, it would not affect the main structure.

Gary: Why do you always do this to me, I thought everything is **done and dusted**. Just send me the detail and I will **take a look**, but there is no guarantee and this is the last time we do this.

託你不要這樣說。文件都簽過了，而且有些部分也開始在生產了。這連臨時修改都算不上唉。

湯瑪士：拜託啦，蓋瑞，這不是什麼大問題，只是一些小小的修改，而且是比較後期才會開始製造的，不會影響主要的結構。

蓋瑞：為什麼你每次都這樣對我，我以為一切都已經講好了。把內容傳給我看看，我不保證可以改，可是這絕對是最後一次。

01 留學生與外派人員

02 上班族

03 異國情侶

04 背包客和觀光客

 **慣用語**

1. the other day　那一天

She mentioned to me **the other day** that the contract would be finalized by end of the month.

他那一天有跟我提過，合約這個月底就會決定。

---

2. last minute　最後一刻、緊要關頭

This **last minute** change is driving me mad, can't you give me more notice?

這種緊要關頭臨時修改的是真的讓我很生氣，難道你不可以提早通知我嗎？

---

3. not a big deal　不是什麼大問題！

Change my shift to the weekend is **not a big deal**, I got nothing on anyway.

把我的班調到周末沒有什麼大問題，反正我也沒事做。

---

4. Why do you always do this to me　你為什麼總是這樣對我

Why do you always do this to me, spent an hour waiting in the rain.

你為什麼總是這樣對我，我在雨中等了你一個小時。

---

5. done and dusted　搞定了、談好了

The statements are all **done and dusted,** I can finally got and get some lunch.

報表都打好了，我終於可以去吃午餐了。

---

6. take a look　看看、評估一下

Can you **take a look** for me of this notice please? Does it mean I can return the goods free of charge?

你幫我看一下這封信好嗎?這樣是代表我可以免費退貨嗎?

---

7. you got to be kidding me　你在開什麼玩笑

What! Shirley is not here again today? **You got to be kidding me!**

什麼!雪莉今天又沒來嗎?你在開玩笑吧!

---

8. make up your mind　你到底要什麼，請決定

We have been in this shop for hours, just make up your mind and grab the one you like!

我們已經在這間店看很久了，你到底要什麼，拿你喜歡的那個就對了。

01 留學生與外派人員

02 上班族

03 異國情侶

04 背包客和觀光客

Unit 21 客戶不守信用

前情提要

Billie 已經跟 Harris 這個客戶催款催了很久。Harris 說好月底要付款，卻還是沒收到款項。

人物角色

● Harris 欠款的客戶
● Billie 會計部的經理

情境對話　　　　MP3 21

Billie: Hello Harris, I am not trying to **stress you out**, but you know the payment we spoke about, we really need it by end of the week.

比利：你好哈里斯，我不是要給你壓力，可是你知道我們談過的那筆帳款，我們的寬限最多只能給到這個禮拜。

Harris: Look, Billie, I know I **missed the deadline**, but you got to know **things are slow** here. I am trying my best to **get by**.

Billie: I understand, we are slow here, too. But I got bills to pay and there are 20 people waiting for their pay cheques. If I don't get this from you we will **go under**. What about some **payment plan**? Half by Friday? You got to **work with me** here.

Harris: I definitely can't do half by Friday, but I will see how much I can **rustle up**.

哈里斯：唉，比利，我知道我又遲了，可是你知道嗎，我們的生意很慘淡，我也很盡力苦撐著。

比利：我懂，我們也是生意不好，可是如果我沒有收到這筆錢我們公司會倒。不然我們讓你分期付款好不好？這個星期五先付一半，你也要幫幫忙啊。

哈里斯：我這星期五真的沒辦法付一半，可是我會盡量湊。

01 留學生與外派人員

02 上班族

03 異國情侶

04 背包客和觀光客

慣用語

1. stress someone out　使某人緊張、加諸壓力

Please don't **stress me out**, I know I struggle to make the credit card payment every month.

不要再讓我緊張了，我知道每個月卡費都繳不太出來。

---

2. miss the deadline　錯過雙方同意的時間

I can't believe I **missed the deadline**. I read the date wrongly.

真不敢相信我遲交了，我看錯日期。

---

3. things are slow　生意很清淡

I don't know how long we can stay open for. **Things are** very **slow** right now.

我不知道我們還可以撐多久，現在生意真的非常不好。

---

4. get by　湊合著過、苦撐

My salary is not much but I manage to **get by** just fine.

我的薪水不高，可是還可以勉強的過。

---

5. go under　生意倒閉

The café around the corner just **went under.** They only stayed open for 6 months.

轉角的咖啡店倒店了，他們只撐了六個月而已。

6. payment plan   分期付款

It will be much appreciated if we could negotiate a better **payment plan**.

如果可以協商出一個更好的還款計畫，我們會很感謝的。

---

7. work with me   配合一下

Why am I doing all the talking, you have to **work with me** here.

為什麼都是我在說，你也要配合一下啊！

---

8 rustle up   湊錢

This is all I can **rustle up** this morning.

我今天早上就只能湊到這麼多。

01 留學生與外派人員

02 上班族

03 異國情侶

04 背包客和觀光客

Unit 22 難纏的客戶

前情提要

客戶藉機殺價，說下訂單卻遲遲不下，問出來的理由是競爭對手提供給他的價格更優惠，他希望我們再降價。

人物角色

● Sean 業務人員
● Hunter 客戶
● Dixon 迪森公司（競爭對手）

情境對話

MP3 22

Sean: Hello Hunter, just want to **follow up** with the order we talked about, can you **give me a rough idea** when it will **come through** please?

西恩：杭特您好，我想追蹤一下我們上一次談過的那個訂單，你可以大概跟我說一下什麼時候會下單嗎？

Hunter: Well, there is a new development, just **between you and me**, Dixon revised their quotation and they are now 2% lower than yours. The board would be **at my throat** if I gave you the order right now.

Sean: You know we have been working together for 5 years, I am always really open with our price. Our price margin is very little, I can try to push the delivery **if that helps.**

Hunter: Delivery is not the issue. What the board wants is to **cut down** the cost. If you can push a bit harder Sean, the order is yours.

Sean: Give me a couple of days to **think about it.**

杭特：嗯，有一些新的變數，偷偷告訴你，迪森公司修改了他們的報價，現在他們比你們的價錢又低了百分之 2。如果我現在下訂單給你，董事會就會跟我吵個沒完。

西恩：你知道我們合作五年了，我們的價錢一直都是很透明的。我們的利潤很少，如果對你有幫助的話，我可以把交期縮短。

杭特：交期不是問題，董事會要的是縮減成本。如果你可以再降一點的話，訂單就是你的了。

西恩：給我幾天時間考慮一下。

01 留學生與外派人員

02 上班族

03 異國情侶

04 背包客和觀光客

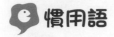慣用語

1. fo.w up　追蹤

What is happening with the new client? Can someone **follow that up** please?

那個新客戶怎麼樣了？誰可以負責追蹤一下？

---

2. give someone a rough idea　跟我大概講一下

I don't know much about our pricing strategy, can you **give me a rough idea** please?

我對我們的價格策略不是很清楚，可以大概跟我講一下嗎？

---

3. come through　有結果

Apparently, they have made the payment, but it just hasn't **come through** yet.

很明顯的他們已經付款了，可是錢還沒進帳。

---

4. between you and me　不要告訴別人

Just **between you and me**, I think the new client is playing us.

不要跟別人說，我覺得這個新客戶在耍我們。

---

5. at someone's (each other's) throat　爭執不休

Can't we just try to be friends, why do we have to be **at each other's throat** all the time?

我們不能和平相處呢？為什麼一定要這樣爭執不休呢？

6. **if that helps**　如果這樣可以幫上你忙的話

Since your car is out of action, I can drive you to work **if that helps.**

既然你的車壞了，如果你需要，我可以載你去上班。

---

7. **cut down**　降低

I think we should car pool. This would **cut down** our patrol cost in half.

我覺得我們應該共乘一部車去上班，這樣油錢可以省一半。

---

8. **think about it**　考慮一下，想像一下

Think about it, how great would it be if we got that order from Mr. Cooper.

想像一下，如果古柏先生把訂單給我們那會有多好。

Unit 23 留言請回電

前情提要

Jenny 這幾天一直在找客戶 Aaron ，打了幾通電話都轉到語音，留言了也沒有回電，Jenny 只好打電話找總機問他的私人手機，打過去給他。Aaron 接到電話但有點不高興因為這是他私人手機。

人物角色

● Emma A 公司業務
● Aaron B 公司經理

情境對話 　　　MP3 23

Aaron: Hello Jenny, How did you get this number?

艾倫：你好珍妮，你怎麼會有我的電話？

Jenny: My apology Aaron, I didn't re-alize you have been **on leave** since

珍妮：對不起打擾你了艾倫，我不曉得你從上個星

last week. The receptionist gave me the number. I got an urgent matter and I had to track you down. I left **a number of** messages and wondering why you didn't **get back to** me.

Aaron: Sorry Jenny, I should have **switched on** the autoreply. I am on holiday at the moment, there is limited email access here. Can I talk to you when I get back on Monday please? **In the meantime**, you can fax the information to me and I promise I will **go through** them all and get back to you on Monday.

Jenny: Thanks Aaron, sorry for interrupting your holiday. **Enjoy it while you can.** Speak to you on Monday.

期就在放假。是公司櫃台小姐給我你的號碼,我有急事找你,我留了很多次訊息給你,可是你一直沒有回我電話。

艾倫:不好意思珍妮,我忘記把自動回覆系統打開。我現在在放假,而且這裡上網不方便。我可以星期一回去再跟你談嗎?有必要的話,你可以先把資料傳真給我,我看過之後星期一再跟你討論。

珍妮:謝謝你艾倫,抱歉打擾你的假期,好好享受,我星期一再跟你談。

01 留學生與外派人員

02 上班族

03 異國情侶

04 背包客和觀光客

 慣用語

1. on leave　放假

I will be **on maternity leave** for a year from next Monday on.

我下星期一開始放一年的育嬰假。

---

2. a number of　一連串的

We received **a number of** complaints against you from our customer.

我們收到一連串針對你的客訴。

---

3. get back to someone　回覆給某人

Make sure you **get back to** Mr. Walcott regarding the tax issues today.

記得今天要回覆沃克先生稅務的問題。

---

4. switch on　開啟

I forgot to **switch on** the alarm last night. We actually got a break-in.

我昨天晚上忘了開防盜器，結果真的有人闖進來。

---

5. in the meantime　這個時候、此時

In the meantime, we can only wait until Declan gets back to know what actually happened.

這個時候我們也只能等戴克倫回來才知道發生什麼事。

6. go through　看過、讀過、翻過

I **went through** everything, but I still couldn't find the piece of paper I am looking for.

我全部都翻過了還是找不到我要找的那張紙。

---

7. enjoy it while you can　好好享受

You deserve a nice holiday, **enjoy it while you can**.

你真的需要去度個假，好好享受

---

8. least of my worries　不需要擔心

There are so much to organise for this trip. What to wear is the **least of my worries.**

關於這個旅程還有很多細節要安排，至於要穿什麼真的不是件重要的事。

Unit 24 背後捅人的同事

前情提要

　　Danielle 剛進這個公司沒多久,他覺得公司同事都很照顧她。直到有一天經理把她叫進辦公室,她覺得經理問的話很奇怪,她才發現其實有人一直在打小報告。

人物角色

- Danielle 公司員工
- Vanessa 公司員工
- Mr. Murdoch 經理

情境對話　　MP3 24

Danielle: Are you aware that the Indonesia project **got taken off** me and now you will be **in charge of** it?

丹妮兒:你知道我負責印尼的那個專案現在不是我做了,換成你負責了嗎?

Vanessa: Well, about that... I did have a word with Mr. Murdoch because he was asking me how are you settling in to the position, I honestly think you are **under a lot of stress** here. Handling 3 projects is just too much for you.

凡妮莎：嗯…有關這件事，我是有跟梅朵先生提過，因為他一直問我妳做得怎麼樣。我是覺得你好像壓力很大，負責三個案子對你來說實在是太多了。

Danielle: What do you mean? I am doing well. I can't believe you **went behind my back**, I thought you were a friend!

丹妮兒：你說什麼！我做得很好，你不要在我背後亂說話，我一直以為你是朋友！

Vanessa: I was just trying to help you out, **take some weight off your shoulders.**

凡妮莎：我只是想幫忙而已，幫你減輕壓力。

Danielle: You already **got your hands full** with 4 projects, what makes you think you can handle more? Take that stupid project if you want, it is **off the cards** for me, but **I don't give a dame.**

丹妮兒：你自己手上忙著四個案子，你還覺得你可以多做就隨便你。反正我是沒戲唱了，可是我才不在乎。

 **慣用語**

1. Got taken off 被奪走，被拿掉

My weekend shifts **got taken off** because the company is trying to cut the cost down.

我週末的班都被取消了因為公司要省錢。

---

2. In charge of 做主，負責

I will be **in charge of** 2 departments once I got promoted to manager.

我升經理之後會開始管理兩個部門。

---

3. Under a lot of stress 壓力很大

Amy is **under a lot of stress** working 7 days a week without a break.

艾咪一個禮拜上七天的班壓力很大。

---

4. Go behind someone's back 在某人背後，偷偷的

Do you know Susan is talking to Claire's boyfriend **behind her back**?

你知道蘇珊偷偷的跟克萊兒的男朋友有聯絡嗎？

---

5. Take some weight off someone's shoulders 幫某人分憂

My dad is working two jobs, I really wish there is something I can do to **take the weight off his shoulders.**

我爸要兼兩份工養家，我真希望有什麼我可以做的來分擔他的辛勞。

6. Got someone's hands full   很忙、很多事要處理

You **got your hands full** with a part-time job and 2 kids.

兩個小孩再加上一份兼職也夠你忙了。

---

7. Off the cards   取消了、玩完了

Don't mention about the new promotion. It is **off the cards** now because they gave it to Rosa instead.

不要再提那個職缺了，沒戲唱了，因為他們決定給羅莎。

---

8. I don't give a dame   不在乎

I don't give a dame about who gets to be the new team leader, as long as he can do a good job.

我不在乎誰升上來當組長，只要他有能力就好。

01 留學生與外派人員

02 上班族

03 異國情侶

04 背包客和觀光客

Unit 25 不做事的同事

前情提要

Lauren 是公司的總機小姐，可是一天到晚都在做自己的事。有時候電話來也不接，還要叫同事接。這天電話響了，她叫 Rebecca 幫她接。

人物角色

- **Lauren** 總機小姐
- **Rebecca** 公司會計

情境對話 ····· `MP3 25`

Lauren: Hey can you just get the phone for me please? I am **in the middle of something** here.

蘿倫：埃，可以幫我接個電話嗎？我現在在忙。

Rebecca: Lauren, I think we need to make it clear here. I am doing the ac-

瑞貝卡：蘿倫，我想跟你澄清一下，我是負責帳務

counts. Answering the phone is not really my job. I can help out **once a while** but lately it just seems like I am **taking over** being a receptionist, too.

Lauren: What's the big deal! I was caught up with something. Most of the calls are for you anyway. I still have to **put it through** to you.

Rebecca: Honestly, if you can just put your mobile phone down, stop texting your friend and update your Facebook status, you will have **plenty of time** to do what you are hired for, just **take it seriously**.

的，接電話不是我的工作，我可以偶而幫個忙，可是最近我好像也要負責櫃台總機。

蘿倫：這有什麼大不了的！我只不過是剛好在忙，反正大部分的電話也都是找你的，省的我還要轉接。

瑞貝卡：說真的，如果你把手機放下，不要再傳簡訊給你的朋友，還有更新臉書的狀態，你就會很有空接電話，拜託認真一點。

 **慣用語** ----------

1. In the middle of something　在忙、走不開

I am **in the middle of something** here, can you go to the meeting for me please?

我現在在忙走不開，可以幫我去開會嗎？

---

2. Once a while　有時候、偶而

We can organise some team bonding activity **once a while.**

偶而我們也可以安排一些團體合作的活動。

---

3. Take over　接手

I am off in 5 minutes, can you **take over** from here?

我在五分鐘就下班了，你可以接手嗎？

---

4. Put it through　轉接

Mr. Bentley is asking for you, can I **put it through**?

班利先生要找你，我可以轉接過去嗎？

---

5. Plenty of time　時間很充裕

If we finished work at 3 everyday, we would have **plenty of time** to exercise.

如果我們每天三點就下班，就不愁沒時間去運動。

---

6. Take it seriously　當一回事

I don't understand how you think this is funny, can you **take it**

seriously please?

我不懂為什麼你會覺得好笑，請你把它當一回事好嗎？

---

7. **call it even**　扯平了，公平

I will pay for dinner tonight, and let's **call it even** since you paid last time.

今天晚餐我付，這樣就公平了，因為上次是你付的。

---

8. **mind your own business**　管好你自己的事就好，別管閒事

Let me alone, **mind your own business.**

不要插手我的事，管好你自己的事就好。

Memo

Unit 26 說錯話

🌸 前情提要

Jess 與 Rosie 是公司同事，這天 Jess 在跟 Rosie 說他最近跟 Nancy 的事

👤 人物角色

- Jess 公司同事
- Rosie 公司同事
- Nancy 公司同事

👄 情境對話 ------- MP3 26

Jessica: Did you notice Nancy's tummy **stick out** like a baby bump?

Rosie: **Come to think of it**, yes she did **put on a lot of weight.**

潔西卡：你有沒有發現南西的肚子凸凸的，像懷孕一樣？

蘿西：仔細想想看好像是，她變胖很多。

Jessica: I thought she was pregnant because I know she has been trying. So, I made a comment about how she has that glow on her face and how cute her baby bump is. It turns out she was not pregnant. I really wanted to **dig a hole and bury myself**. I can't believe I **made a total fool out of myself**. I was so embarrassed, I couldn't **look at her in the eye**.

Rosie: You must be **out of your mind**! That is so funny! I can't believe you did that to her!

Jessica: Speak of the devil, here she comes.

潔西卡：我以為她懷孕了因為我知道她一直想生，所以我跟她說她有孕媽媽的好氣色而且肚子很可愛。結果她根本沒懷孕，我當下只想挖一個洞跳進去。真不敢相信我出這麼大的洋相，真是太丟臉了，我根本不敢抬頭看她。

蘿西：你真的是瘋了，這太好笑了。我不敢相信你對她說了那種話。

潔西卡：說人人到，她來了。

01 留學生與外派人員

02 上班族

03 異國情侶

04 背包客和觀光客

 **慣用語**

1. stick out 凸出來、突出的

It is good to be that tall. He **sticks out** among everybody.

長得高真好，他在人群中很突出。

---

2. come to think of it 仔細想想看

I never really thought of him that way, but **come to think of it**, he really is a genius.

我從來沒有這樣看待他，可是仔細想想，他真的是個天才。

---

3. put on weight 變胖

I am trying so hard to lose weight, I **put on so much weight** over the past two months.

我在試著減肥，我過去兩個月內胖了很多。

---

4. dig a hole and bury oneself 挖個洞跳進去（很丟臉的意思）

I wanted to **dig a hole and bury myself** when I found out he was listening to our conversation next door.

當我發現他在隔壁房間聽到我們的對話時，我真的想挖個洞跳進去。

---

5. make a fool out of oneself 出洋相，讓某人難看

He totally **made a fool out of himself** by taking his shirt off and dance on the table.

他真的出洋相到了極點，怎麼會想到要把上衣脫掉站到桌上跳舞。

6. look at someone in the eye 直視某人

I think it is very rude if you don't **look at the person in the eye** when you are speaking to them.

我覺得當你跟人家講話的時候，不直視對方是一種很沒禮貌的行為。

---

7. out of someone's mind 瘋了、沒想清楚

She must be **out of her mind** to pick Dick to be her boyfriend.

她一定是瘋了才會選迪克當她男朋友。

---

8. speaking of the devil 說人人到

Speaking of the devil, Zoe just walked in the room.

說人人到，若儀剛剛走進來。

Unit 27 上司不採納你的意見

前情提要

公司決定要合併底下子公司的幾個部門以節省支出，**Dylan** 覺得很不妥，想與上司溝通是不是有其他方式

人物角色

- Dylan 下屬
- Taylor 上司

情境對話　　MP3 27

Dylan: I don't know why you decided to **go ahead with** that restructure in such a hurry. I don't think it was properly **thought through**.

Taylor: What makes you said that?

狄倫：我不知道為什麼你要這麼匆促的決定這個重整計畫，我覺得還需要深思熟慮過。

泰勒：為什麼你這麼說？

Dylan: Imagine how many people would be **laid-off.**

狄倫：想想看有多少人會被解僱。

Taylor: Don't be so naive. You should **think big**. You would be laughing when you got that big fat bonus.

泰勒：不要太天真，你應該往大處著眼。等你領到大份的紅利你就只會記得笑了。

Dylan: The idea just doesn't **sit right with** me. I am sure we would come out with a **win-win** solution if we have more time.

狄倫：對於這個計畫我覺得心很不安，我覺得只要有更多的時間，我們一定可以想出一個雙贏的辦法。

Taylor: If we don't act quickly, we **don't stand a chance**. The Lee group has been planning the same idea for a long time.

泰勒：如果我們不趕快進行的話，我們就沒有贏面了。李氏公司早就一直在計畫同樣的事了。

Dylan: I know you **have your mind made up** and there is nothing I can do about it.

狄倫：我知道你早就決定要做了，我也沒有辦法改變。

01 留學生與外派人員

02 上班族

03 異國情侶

04 背包客和觀光客

 慣用語

1. go ahead with something　進行某件事

We decide to **go ahead with** putting down a deposit for the apartment we viewed last week.

上星期去看過的那間公寓，我們決定要下訂金了。

---

2. thought through　想得很清楚、深思熟慮

The plan is properly **thought through.** We took a lot of advice from a professional consultant.

這個計畫縝密的計畫過，我們集合了很多專業顧問的意見。

---

3. lay-off　解雇、辭職

I can't believe the company decided to **lay off** 10 % of the employees.

我不敢相信公司決定解雇一成的員工。

---

4. think big　考慮遠景、往大處著眼

We start small, but we **think big**.

我們先從小規模做起，可是我們有長遠的打算。

---

5. sit right with someone　讓某人覺得安心、放心

Knowing what he can possibly do, the idea does not **sit right with me**.

因為了解他的性格，這個計畫讓我很不安心。

6. **win-win**　雙贏

I think this is a **win-win** situation, you get to expand your company, and the contractors got their job back.

我覺得這是雙贏的局面，你既可以擴展營業，承包商也有工作做。

---

7. **don't stand a chance**　沒有贏面、一定輸的

Compared with Jeremy's background, you **don't stand a chance.**

如果是跟傑若米的背景比起來，你一點贏面都沒有。

---

8. **have your mind made up**　決定了

Let me know what you want me to do once you **have your mind made up.**

你決定好了再告訴我怎麼做就可以了。

Unit 28 上班遲到

🗯 前情提要

Samuel 是快遞公司的員工個性很散漫，最近常因私事而遲到。老闆 Barry 已經快忍受不了。然而他今天早上又遲到了，老闆看到他進來就破口大罵！

👤 人物角色

● **Barry** 快遞公司老闆
● **Samuel** 員工

👄 情境對話

`MP3 28`

Barry: <u>Where the hell have you been</u>? You are an hour late!

巴瑞：你跑到哪裡去了？遲到一個小時了。

Samuel: Hmmm....There was an ac-

山姆：嗯，高速公路上出

cident on the highway, and the traffic was really **backed up**.

了車禍，所以很塞車。

Barry: Why didn't you call? You could have called and let us know. You know the orders have to go out by 7 am otherwise it won't get there in time. I had customers calling the whole morning to complain. I am really **fed up** with this.

巴瑞：為什麼你不打個電話來通知？你可以早點通知我們的！你知道訂單在七點前全部都要送出去，不然來不及。我正個早上都在接客戶抱怨的電話，我受夠了。

Samuel: I am really sorry. I promise **it won't happen again**.

山姆：我很抱歉，我保證不再犯了。

Barry: This is getting ridiculous now. I can't **put our reputation at risk.**

巴瑞：這現在越來越可笑。我不能讓我們名聲蒙受風險。

Samuel: I know, I know. I haven't been reliable lately, but I promise I will be on time **from now on**. The orders will go out **first thing in the morning**.

山姆：我知道，我知道，我最近一直出狀況，我保證我現在開始一定會準時。訂單我一定優先處理。

Barry: Well, **actions speak louder than words**, prove it to me.

巴瑞：嗯！不要空口說白話，證明給我看。

01 留學生與外派人員

02 上班族

03 異國情侶

04 背包客和觀光客

 慣用語

1. **where have you been?** 你跑到哪裡去了？

We looked all over for you, **where have you been?**

我們到處找你，你到哪去了？

---

2. **back up** 塞車、阻塞、支援、備份

There are only a few people serving at ticketing counter, the queue is **backing up.**

售票口只有幾個人在服務，排隊的隊伍越來越長。

---

3. **fed up** 受夠了

I am **fed up** with all the excuses you come out with.

我受夠你的藉口了。

---

4. **won't happen again** 保證不會再發生、下次不敢了

I apologize for my mistake, I swear it **won't happen again.**

對於我的錯誤，我很抱歉。我保證下次不會再犯了。

---

5. **put something/someone at risk** 使某事或某人冒風險

By letting her go out there alone, you are **putting her safety at risk.**

你讓她自己一個人去，那就是不把她的人身安全當一回事

---

6. **from now on** 從現在開始

I promise I will be more careful **from now on.**

我保證從現在開始我會小心一點。

---

7. first thing in the morning　一到就要做、第一件做的事

I know this is an urgent matter. I will contact Mr. Robertson **first thing in the morning.**

我知道這是急事，我明天一早就馬上跟羅伯森先生連絡。

---

8. actions speak louder than words　不要空口說白話

You made a lot of promises, but I believe **actions speak louder than words.**

你隨口答應了很多事情，可是我相信行動可以證明一切。

Memo

Unit 29 忘記上司交代的事

 前情提要

派瑞一早就收到老闆給他的警告信，他覺得很沮喪，現在在跟同事吐苦水。

 人物角色

- Perry 犯錯的員工
- Greg Johnson 老闆
- Luke 同事

情境對話 MP3 29

Perry: I got my 2nd warning from Greg Johnson today, what a terrible way to start a day.

派瑞：我今天收到桂格強森給的警告信，已經是第二份了。今天怎麼一早就這麼倒楣。

Luke: You got to be kidding, **what for**?

路克：開玩笑地吧！是為了什麼？

Perry: He asked me to **look after** the client last Friday, but I forgot to organise the pick-up for him. The client was upset and Greg is really **pissed off** with me right now.

派瑞：他叫我負責上星期五的客戶拜訪，可是我忘了安排接機。客戶真的很不高興，所以杜格現在很氣我。

Luke: Oh, no. That's terrible. You know how much Greg values client relations. You are lucky you didn't get fired **on the spot.** You really need to **get your act together.**

路克：喔，那真的很慘，你知道杜格很注重客戶關係的，你算很幸運，沒有當場被炒魷魚。你真的要用心一點。

Perry: It was a silly mistake. But I need to be **on my best behaviour** and **lay low** for a while. I can't afford to make any more mistakes, otherwise I will be gone **in no time**.

派瑞：這真的是很蠢的錯誤，我真的要發條上緊一點，暫時低調行事。不能再犯錯了，不然我應該很快就被炒了。

 慣用語

1. what for　為了什麼

Thanks for the present but **what is this for?**

謝謝你的禮物，可是是為了什麼原因送我呢？

---

2. look after　負責、照顧

I will be **looking after** you during your visit here.

你的旅程都會由我安排照顧。

---

3. pissed off　生氣

I don't know how she can possibly mess up the two clients, I am so **pissed off** with her right now.

我不了解她怎麼可以把兩個客戶搞錯，我真的很氣她。

---

4. on the spot　當場

I got caught by a police man for speeding, I got a ticket **on the spot.**

我超速被警察攔下來，他當場開罰單給我。

---

5. get your act together　專注、認真、好好表現

Can you just focus and **get your act together** please?

可不可以專心下來好好表現？

---

6. on someone's best behaviour　發條上緊一點、表現好一點

The manager will be keeping an eye on Ada in the next a few

months. She really needs to be **on her best behaviour.**

這幾個月經理都會小心留意艾達，她真的需要表現好一點。

---

7. lay low 低調

I am on his watch list, I think the best thing for me to do is to **lay low** for a while.

我知道他在注意我，我覺得最好的處理方式就最近低調一點

---

8. in no time 馬上

Give me a call when you need me, I will be here **in no time.**

需要我的時候就打給我，我會馬上到。

Memo

#%V*拜①i

129

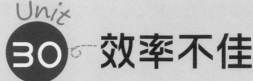

 前情提要

Mitch 聽到公司的風聲說老闆準備修理 Andrew，他偷偷先跟 Andrew 警告。

人物角色

- Mitch 聽到風聲的同事
- Charlie 老闆
- Andrew 同事

情境對話   MP3 30

Mitch: You'd better **watch out**, I heard Charlie is upset with you because you didn't meet the sales target. He is going to grill you **like nothing else**. You'd better **be ready for it**.

米契：你最好小心一點，我聽說查理對你很感冒，因為你沒有達到業務目標。他會狠狠地拷問你，你最好有心理準備。

Andrew: oh, **give me a break**, I only just started last month and still **finding my way around**. I am just a **new kid on the block**. He is just asking too much.

Mitch: My advice is to push yourself harder, you really need to be **on top of your game** to get ahead in this company. You got to know there are people lining up to get the opportunity you got given.

Andrew: I know what you mean. I'd better come out with a good answer before he **skins me alive.**

安德魯：天哪，有沒有必要這樣，我上個月才進公司，還在適應中。我不過是新來的，他的要求也太高了吧！

米契：我的建議是你要努力一點，在這間公司你要比別人更傑出，才有機會升職。你要了解有多少人等著想進我們公司。

安德魯：我了解，我最好想一個好答案，不然他會把我活活剝一層皮！

01 留學生與外派人員

02 上班族

03 異國情侶

04 背包客和觀光客

💬 慣用語

1. watch out 小心

I need to **watch out** for the catches. I don't want to make more mistakes.

我需要小心那些陷阱，我不能再出錯了。

---

2. like nothing else 極度的、極端的、瘋狂的

She can scream **like nothing else** when she is upset.

她不高興的時候會瘋狂的大叫

---

3. be ready for it 準備好

I heard the big news is coming. You'd better **be ready for it**!

我聽說有天大的事情要發生，你最好做好準備！

---

4. give me a break 有沒有必要這樣、不要逼我

Come on **give me a break**, I know I will find a way to deal with it sooner or later.

拜託不要再逼我，我遲早會想出方法的。

---

5. finding my way around 還在習慣中

I am still **finding my way around** the neighbourhood since I only just moved here.

我才剛搬到這區，我還在習慣中。

---

6. new kid on the block 新來的

It is a lot of pressure being the **new kid on the block,** people are always watching you.

當新來的人蠻有壓力的，因為每個人都會注意你。

---

7. on top of someone's game　比別人傑出

Steven is really **on top of his game.** He has been the sales of the month since March.

史蒂芬真的很強，自從三月份起他每個月都是業務冠軍。

---

8. skin someone alive　被罵到臭頭、活活剝一層皮

Look at this mess, my wife is going to **skin me alive** if I don't clean it up before she gets home.

看看這裡這麼亂，如果我老婆回來之前沒收好，我會被她罵死。

前情提要

經理在年初跟 Brian 提過加薪這回事，可是等了大半年都沒有消息。Brian 跟女朋友打算買房子，他想再去跟上司問一下。

👤 人物角色

- Brian 員工
- Henry 上司

💋 情境對話 　　　　　　MP3 31

Brian: I don't want to **beat around the bush,** I just want to know that pay rise you mentioned at the beginning of the year, is it still **on the table**? I **can really use a bit of** extra

布萊恩：我就直接講了，我想知道一下你年初提過的加薪，現在還有機會嗎？我真的需要一點額外的錢，因為我們計畫付房

money now. We are planning to **put down** a deposit for a house.

Henry: Well, about that, you know we are undergoing the restructure. The board is putting the pay rise **on hold** for now.

Brian: You know I have been with the company **forever and a day.** I **pulled in** a lot of profit for you and I think I deserve it a fair share. Do you think you can **put in a few good words** for me at the board meeting?

子的訂金。

亨利：嗯，談到那個問題，你知道公司現在正在重組，董事會決定暫時停止加薪。

布萊恩：你也知道我在公司很久了，也幫公司賺了很多錢，我覺得加薪是我應得的。董事會的時候可以幫我說説好話嗎？

慣用語

1. beat around the bush 旁敲側擊

Stop **beating around the bush,** just being straight forward with me.

別再旁敲側擊了，有話直接跟我説。

2. on the table 還有嗎？還在嗎？還有機會嗎？

You know that new position in R&D, is it still **on the table**? I am keen to apply.

那個研發部的新職務還要請人嗎？我想申請。

3. can use a bit of / some of 需要某樣東西或幫助

Are you free? I **can really use a bit of** help now.

你有空了嗎？我需要人幫忙 。

4. put down 付款、付訂金

How much do we have to **put down** as the deposit?

訂金要付多少？

5. on hold 暫停、等待

Sorry I am on the other line, can I put you **on hold** please?

不好意思我在接另一線的電話，可以麻煩您稍等嗎？

6. forever and a day 很久了

The promotion has finally come through, I waited **forever and**

136

a day！

等了好久我終於升職了！

---

7. **pull in** 帶入

How much profit did you **pull in** last month?

上個月你幫公司賺了多少錢？

---

8. **put in good words** 說好話

Can you **put in some good words** for me? I am trying to get on Henry's good side.

可不可以幫我說說好話？我想讓亨利比較喜歡我一點。

Memo

 前情提要

　　喬許是公司的資深員工，他知道最近公司的分行經理剛退休，他很有可能被升職。他的上司很支持他，說會盡力幫忙，可是結果很他失望。

人物角色

- Josh 員工
- Roger 上司
- Rachel Yates 執行長的女兒

情境對話　　MP3 32

Josh: Where is the promotion you promised me Roger? I got the company announcement to congratulate Rachel Yates as the new branch man-

喬許：你答應我的升職呢羅傑？我收到公司的郵件說恭喜瑞秋葉茲成為新任分行經理，到底在搞什

ager. **What the hell is happening here** !

Roger: I know Josh, I've done what I can, but I **have no say** in this. The board overturn my recommendation. You always know Rachel **has the upper hand.**

Josh: You are telling me I **worked my ass off** for this company for 15 years, and now it is **back to square one** for some CEO's daughter!

Roger: Look, there will be other opportunities for you **sooner or later,** you just need to be patient.

Josh: That's it! I am out of here. I **had enough** of this bullshit.

麼！

羅傑：我懂，羅傑，我已經盡力了，可是我沒有決定權。董事會否定我的建議，你知道瑞秋本來就比較佔優勢。

喬許：你是說我為了公司辛苦付出 15 年，現在因為什麼執行長的女兒又回到了原點！

羅傑：不要這樣，遲早都會有其他機會的。你的耐心。

喬許：算了，我辭職，受夠這些狗屁了。

 慣用語 ················•

1. what the hell is happening　這到底是怎麼回事

This place is a mess, **what the hell is happening**?

這個地方亂到不行，到底發生什麼事？

---

2. have no say　沒有決定權

My girlfriend picks out what I wear every day. I **have no say** in it

我每天穿什麼都是我女朋友決定的，我沒得選。

---

3. has the upper hand　有優勢的

I think we **have the upper hand here.** We got the advantage of working with the account department.

我覺得我們很佔優勢，因為我們會跟會計部一起。

---

4. work one's ass off　辛苦付出

Morris **worked his ass off** to have the project finish on time. What an amazing job he has done!

莫里斯為了準時完成這個案子付出很多，但是實在做的很棒！

---

5. back to square one　回到原點

I lost all the data I was working on in a blackout last night. Now I am **back to square one.**

昨天晚上突然停電我的資料都不見了，現在要從頭開始。

6. **sooner or later**　遲早

As long as you keep trying, I am sure you will make it **sooner or later.**

只要你不要放棄，你遲早都會成功。

---

7. **that's it**　好了、就這樣了

That's it! That is exactly what I wanted.

這樣就對了！我想要的就是這樣。

---

8. **had enough**　受夠了

She keeps going on and on about how terrible her boyfriend is, I **had enough** listening to that crap.

她一直不停的說她男朋友有多糟，我真的是聽夠了。

01 留學生與外派人員

02 上班族

03 異國情侶

04 背包客和觀光客

Unit 33 被迫加班

 **前情提要**

Peter 剛剛接任經理，很心急想做很多事。這天他又來叫員工加班。

 人物角色

- Ryan 公司員工
- Peter 新任經理

情境對話 MP3 33

Peter: I need a favour Ryan. These reports need to be done before the 9 am meeting tomorrow morning.

彼得：我需要幫忙，萊恩！這些報告需要在明天早上九點開會之前趕出來。

Ryan: Come on Peter, this is the 3rd night **in a row** we have to stay back.

萊恩：天啊！彼得，這是連續第三天叫我們留下來

Can't you just **push** the meeting **back** for a day, so we don't need to **burn the midnight oil** again?

了，你不能把會議推遲一天嗎？這樣我們就不用又要熬夜了。

Peter: **Take one for the team** Ryan, I know you can do it. Take some time off after we **get through** this, but we really need you at this moment before the financial year ends.

彼得：就靠你了萊恩，我知道你可以的。等我們忙完這一波後你請幾天假休息吧！可是這個時候在會計年度結束之前我們真的很需要你。

Ryan: What can I say, do I have a choice?

萊恩：我又能說什麼呢？我有選擇嗎？

Peter: Thanks Ryan, **I owe you one**.

彼得：太感謝你了萊恩，我欠你一個人情。

Ryan: You need to **get a life**, you **worry about nothing but** work.

萊恩：你真的需要享受一下人生，你的眼裡只有工作。

 慣用語

1. **in a row** 連續

Having chicken for dinner 3 nights **in a row** really turns me off.

連續三天晚餐都吃雞肉我都沒胃口了。

---

2. **push something back** 推遲

I have to **push my doctor appointment back** because an incident happened at work.

因為公司出了一點事，我只好把原本的門診預約延後。

---

3. **burn the midnight oil** 熬夜

My body just couldn't handle it if I keep **burning the midnight oil.**

我如果不停的熬夜身體會受不了。

---

4. **take one for the team** 就靠你了

You are the best IT guy we got, just **take one for the team.** I know you will do well.

你是我們最棒的電腦工程師，就派你去了，我知道你會很棒的。

---

5. **get through** 經歷、度過

I know the situation is difficult, but as long as we work together, we will **get through** it.

我知道現在情況不好，可是只要我們一起合作，我們會撐過去的。

6. **I owe you one** 欠你一個人情

Thanks for not telling my girlfriend where I was last night, **I owe you one.**

謝謝你昨天沒有跟我女朋友說我在哪裡，我欠你一個人情。

---

7. **get a life** 生活太無趣、享受生活、不要管這些無聊的事

If you are upset about how the towels need to be folded, I think you really need to go and **get a life.**

如果你連毛巾要怎麼摺這種小事都要管，那你的生活真的是太無趣了！

---

8. **worry about nothing but...** 只擔心⋯

You **worry about nothing but** money all the time. I think you forgot what a girlfriend is for.

你一天到晚只擔心錢，你都不知道女朋友是要來幹嘛的！

01 留學生與外派人員

02 上班族

03 異國情侶

04 背包客和觀光客

Unit

34 想換工作

 **前情提要**

Renee 和 Damien 是公司同事，私交也很好。這天 Renee 在跟 Damien 抱怨公司一直都不讓他升職。

 人物角色

- Renee 公司同事
- Damien 公司同事

情境對話 ⌐⌐⌐⌐⌐⌐⌐⌐⌐⌐ MP3 34

Renee: I think I have reached my limit. I can do it **with my eyes closed**.

雷娜：我覺得我已經達到一個瓶頸，這份工作我已經學得差不多了。

Damien: Have you **put in** an appli-

戴米恩：你有沒有想申請

cation for an internal transfer to a different department?

Renee: of course I did, I applied a few managerial positions and other more challengeable roles but it just **went nowhere**. I have been stuck being an admin officer for 3 years. Doing the same thing over and over is **doing my head in.**

Damien: I think you should start **looking around**

Renee: You know I am **up for** new challenges, I wish they would **take a chance on me.** Maybe it is time for **a fresh start.**

內部調職到不同的單位？

雷娜：當然有，我申請了幾個管理階層的職位還有一些比較有挑戰性的職務，可是都沒結果。我已經當了三年的文書了，重複做同樣的事我都快發瘋了。

戴米恩：我覺得你應該開始留意別的工作機會。

雷娜：你知道的，我喜歡接受新的挑戰，我多希望他們能夠給我機會。也許是時候到了，要換跑道了。

 慣用語

1. with one's eyes closed　閉著眼睛都會做

I am so familiar with the new dance routine. I can do it **with my eye's closed.**

新的舞步我已經很熟了，熟到閉著眼睛都會跳。

---

2. put in　申請

I am still unsure about whether to **put in** an application for the new position.

我還在考慮是不是要申請那個新的職位。

---

3. go nowhere　沒消息、沒有結果

I have told Gordon more than once that this needed to be amended, but it just **goes nowhere.**

我不只一次告訴高登這個部分需要修改，可是一直都沒有下文。

---

4. doing one's head in　發瘋了、受不了

Danny keeps making the same mistakes. It is **doing my head in.**

丹尼一直犯相同的錯誤，我快要受不了了。

---

5. looking around　留意

I am **looking around** for other opportunities to do my internship.

我在找是不是有別的地方可以讓我實習。

6. up for　有興趣、可以接受

I heard you are looking for someone to take part in that new project, just to let you know I am **up for** it.

我聽說你在找人參與這個新的專案，我想跟你說我很有興趣。

---

7. take a chance on someone　給某人一次機會

I think you should **take a chance on** Mick. He seems like a nice guy.

我覺得你應該給米克一次機會，他看起來是個不錯的男生。

---

8. a fresh start　一個新開始

I moved here because I wanted **a fresh start**.

我搬來這裡是因為我想要有個新開始。

Unit 35 其他公司來挖角

 前情提要

Jasper 決定要離開該目前任職的公司，他想在正式提出辭呈之前先跟他的上司打聲招呼。

人物角色

- Jasper 員工
- Curtis 公司經理

情境對話

MP3 35

Jasper: I don't think there is any easier way to say this, but I was approached by a **head hunter,** apparently Pacific bank would like to **have me on board** as their new branch manager in Sydney.

賈斯柏：我不知道該怎麼跟你說，有一間獵人頭公司找上我，説太平洋銀行想要我擔任他們雪梨的分行經理。

Curtis: Right... Hmmm... what do you plan to do?

科特斯：喔！這樣嗎…那你打算怎麼做？

Jasper: I've given a serious thought about this, and I decided to take it. I mean it is **once in a life time** opportunity. I just want you to be the first one to know before it is official.

賈斯柏：我很認真考慮了，我決定要接受那個職位。你也知道這是畢生難得的好機會。我只希望在我公開之前先跟你打聲招呼。

Curtis: Thanks for the **heads up**. It would be sad to lose a good worker like you. I mean, what do they offer? We might be able to **top it**! We can always **work something out** for you.

科特斯：謝謝你提前跟我說，失去像你一樣的好員工會很令人失望。我想說，他們到底給你什麼福利？我們可能可以加碼！我們可以好好談談。

Jasper: Their offer **ticked all the boxes**, I don't think you can even **match it**.

賈斯柏：他們的條件都是對我有吸引力的東西，我覺得你可能連提出一樣的條件都很難。

 慣用語

1. head hunter　獵人頭公司，人力仲介

I always wonder how the **head hunters** pick their candidates.

我一直在想獵人頭公司都是怎樣挑人的。

---

2. have someone on board　聘僱、加入

Would you consider to come and work with me? It will be great to **have you on board.**

你有興趣來幫我工作嗎？如果有你加入我們的團隊會更棒。

---

3. once in a life time　難得的

The house I've always wanted is finally for sale. It is **once in a life time** opportunity.

我一直想要的那間房子終於要賣了，這是難得的機會。

---

4. heads up　預先警告

Thanks for the **heads up,** I avoided the confrontation with Nelson this morning.

謝謝你的小道消息，我早上特意避開跟尼爾森對槓。

---

5. top it　超過、更好

I know they are offering you $30 dollars an hour, but I can **top it** if you willing to stay.

我知道他們願意給你每小時 30 塊，如果你願意留下來的話，我一定會加碼。

6. work something out 安排、商量

I know you need to leave early to pick up your kids, I am sure we can **work something out** for you.

我知道你要提早離開去接小孩，我們可以商量一下最好的安排。

---

7. tick all the boxes 符合期望的、無法挑剔的

This guy's portfolio is amazing. He **ticks all the boxes.**

這個男人的學經歷真是太完美了，真是無法挑剔。

---

8. match it 提出一樣的條件、配合

I must say the offer is too good to be true. I can barely **match it.**

我必須要同意他們提出的條件真的很好，我根本沒辦法跟他們比。

Unit 36 討論不想做的事

 前情提要

公司最近要擴張業務部門，決定將部分員工轉到業務部。**Johnny** 算是一個內向的人，聽到這個消息，心裡已經有種排斥感。沒想到今天經理就找他聊聊。

 人物角色

- *Craig* 公司經理
- *Adam* 員工
- *Tina* 員工

 情境對話 `MP3 36`

Craig: What do you think of taking up a sales role? We really need to **boost up** our sales figure.

奎格： 你覺得調到業務部怎麼樣？我們真的需要增加我們的銷售額。

Adam: Me!? Doing sales? You got to be kidding. Sales is really **not my thing**. You know I am not a people person. I **freak out** whenever I need to speak to someone I don't know. I can't do it. It is too **full on**.

Craig: I think as long as you **come out of your shell** a bit more, you will be fine! You know we will **train you up**.

Adam: Honestly, this is not what I signed up for Craig. Can't you just let me be?

Craig: You don't have to **rush into** any decision right now. Go home and **sleep on it**, trust me it is not all that bad. You will be on base salary plus commission.

Adam: I think you should talk to Tina about it. She will make a wonderful sales.

亞當：你説我嗎？當業務？不要開玩笑了！我真的不適合，你知道我不會跟人家相處。我只要跟陌生人講話就會緊張，我沒辦法啦！壓力太大了！

奎格：我覺得只要你放開一點，你就可以了！我們也會提供訓練的。

亞當：説實話，這真的不是我想要的，你不能讓我做我現在的職務就好了嗎？

奎格：你不用現在急著決定，回家好好想一想，相信我這真的沒有那麼糟。你是領底薪加傭金。

亞當：我覺得你應該跟緹娜談談，她會很適合當業務。

慣用語

1. boost up 提升、增加

The best way to **boost up** your confidence is to take up a new challenge.

提升自信的最好方法就是接受一個新的挑戰。

---

2. not someone's thing 不合我胃口、不適合

I am a home body, those outdoor activities are just **not my thing**.

我喜歡宅在家，戶外活動不和我胃口。

---

3. freak out 嚇壞了

Penny totally **freaked out** when the car just came out from nowhere.

那台車不知道從哪裡衝出來的，潘妮真的嚇壞了。

---

4. full on 很有壓力的、讓人緊張的

The sales training was very **full on**, they put a lot of pressure on me.

銷售員的訓練很讓人緊張，他們讓我覺得壓力很大。

---

5. come out of someone's shell 放開一點、不要害羞

I think it would take a long time for Vicky to **come out of her shell**.

我覺得要很長一段時間薇琪才會不那麼拘謹。

6. train someone up　訓練

I am not a good public speaker and I wish someone could **train me up** for it.

我不擅長公眾演說，我真希望有人可以訓練我。

---

7. rush into　急著、衝動

Don't **rush into** buying a car, you really need to know what you want it for.

不要太衝動買車，你要想一下你要這台車做什麼。

---

8. sleep on it　好好考慮

Benjamin never makes the decision on the spot. He always goes home and **sleep on it** before he came to the decision.

班傑明從來不會當下做出決定，他一定會回家好好考慮再決定。

篇章回顧

精選慣用語

1. have a word　談談

I need to **have a word** with you regarding the latest company policy.

我需要跟你談談最新的公司規定

----

2. rustle up　湊錢

This is all I can **rustle up** this morning.

我今天早上就只能湊到這麼多。

----

3. Take some weight off someone's shoulders　幫某人分憂

My dad is working two jobs, I really wish there is something I can do to **take the weight off his shoulders.**

我爸要兼兩份工養家，我真希望有什麼我可以做的來分擔他的辛勞。

----

4. Off the cards　取消了、玩完了

Don't mention about the new promotion, it is **off the cards** now because they gave it to Rosa instead.

不要再提那個職缺了，沒戲唱了，因為他們決定給羅莎。

---

5. **sit right with someone** 讓某人覺得安心、放心

Knowing what he can possibly do, the idea does not **sit right with me**.

因為了解他的性格，這個計畫讓我很不安心。

---

6. **don't stand a chance** 沒有贏面、一定輸的

Compare with Jeremy's background, you **don't stand a chance**.

如果是跟傑若米的背景比起來，你一點贏面都沒有。

---

7. **get your act together** 專注、認真、好好表現

Can you just focus and **get your act together** please?

可不可以專心下來好好表現？

---

8. **skin someone alive** 被罵到臭頭、活活剝一層皮

Look at this mess, my wife is going to **skin me alive** if I don't clean it up before she gets home.

看看這裡這麼亂，如果我老婆回來之前沒收好，我會被她罵死。

PART **03**
異國情侶

學習進度表

看完的單元也別忘了打勾喔！！

Unit 37 約會遲到

前情提要

David 跟 Talia 剛認識，今天兩個人約在電影院要去看電影，電影已經開始了可是 David 一直還沒到，Talia 打手機也沒人接，正在想要怎麼辦時，David 終於到了，可是 Talia 已經很不爽了。

人物角色

- David 想追 Talia 的男生
- Talia 女主角

情境對話　　MP3 37

David: I am so sorry, I **meant to** get here before you but I have no idea here I put my keys and I left my phone at home. Just let me get the tickets quickly before the movie starts.

大衛：真是對不起，我是打算要比你早到的，可是我找不到我的鑰匙，而且把電話忘在家裡。在電影開始前，先讓我去買票。

Talia: **By the time** we get in the movie would be **half way through**. **Forget about it.** Let's just go.

塔莉亞：等我們進去電影都演到一半了，算了，我們走啦。

David: I know it is my fault, please **don't be like that.**

大衛：我知道是我的錯，不要這樣好不好。

Talia: You really need to **be more organized** next time. I wasn't sure whether you are coming or not. I thought you **stood me up**.

塔莉亞：你下次真的不能這樣糊里糊塗，我根本不知道你有沒有要來，我以為你放我鴿子。

David: I feel really bad, please tell me what I can do to **make it up to** you. Let me take you somewhere nice for dinner as my apology.

大衛：我真的很抱歉，拜託你跟我說怎樣可以補償你，我們找一間好一點的餐廳吃晚餐算我跟你賠罪好不好。

01 留學生與外派人員

02 上班族

03 異國情侶

04 背包客和觀光客

慣用語

1. meant to 故意的、有心的

I didn't **meant to** miss your call. It was on silent and I didn't hear it.

我不是故意不接妳電話，我把它轉靜音，沒有聽到。

---

2. by the time 到時候

By the time we found parking, it would be time to go home.

等我們找到車位可能天都黑了。

---

3. half way through 中途、過一半

Can we talk later please? I am **half way through** the movie.

可以等一下再說嗎？我電影看到一半。

---

4. forget about it 算了

This plan is just not working. **Forget about it**. Let's just start again.

這個計畫行不通，算了，我們從頭開始好了。

---

5. don't be like that 不要這樣嘛

Please **don't be like that**, I don't know what I have done wrong.

不要這樣嘛，我不知道我做錯什麼。

---

6. be more organized 不要那麼糊里糊塗

Don't forget to pack your underwear this time, please **be**

more organized.

這次不要再忘記帶內褲了，不要那麼糊里糊塗。

---

7. **stand someone up** 放某人鴿子

I can't believe he **stood me up.** I didn't even like him that much.

我不敢相信他居然放我鴿子，我根本對他沒什麼興趣。

---

8. **make it up to someone** 補償某人

I am not sure how to **make it up to** her. I broke her favorite cup by accident.

我不知道該怎麼補償她，我不小心把她最喜歡的茶杯打破了。

Memo

Unit 38 一起去度假

 前情提要

William 是個很粗線條的人，Grace 一手計畫跟他一起到泰國旅行，交代他要帶些保暖的衣服因為泰國北部比較涼爽。他卻沒聽 Grace 的建議，只帶了短袖衣物，Grace 實在受不了他的少根筋，因為不是第一次了。

人物角色

- William 男朋友
- Grace 女朋友

情境對話 ⟶ MP3 38

William: it is a bit chilly here. I wish I brought a jacket with me.

威廉：這裡有點冷，我真希望我有帶外套。

Grace: What! You didn't bring one!?

葛蕾斯：什麼！你沒有

Why am I not surprised. I did remind you to pack some warm clothes, but you just never **take my words seriously**.

William: I thought Thailand was supposed to be hot **all year round**. This is totally **out of my expectation.**

Grace: I don't know **what's wrong with you**. I told you "northern" Thailand. It gets cold at night I swear you **live in la-la land** sometimes.

William: Please don't **be mad at me**. This is **an easy fix.** All I have to do is to go down to the shops to get a jacket. I don't want to spoil the trip for you by not having the right clothes.

帶！？為什麼我一點都不驚訝呢！我有提醒你要帶保暖衣物，可是你從來不把我説的話當一回事。

威廉：我以為泰國一年四季都是很熱的，這真是出乎我意料之外。

葛蕾斯：我真不懂你是哪根筋不對，我跟你説泰國「北部」晚上會冷。我真的覺得你有時候太搞不清楚狀況了！

威廉：不要生我的氣嘛，這很容易解決啊，我只要去買件夾克就好。我不想要因為帶錯衣服，讓你玩得不盡興。

 慣用語

1. why am I not surprised　為什麼我一點都不意外

You spilled the beer? **Why am I not surprised**, you do that every time.

你翻倒啤酒？為什麼我一點都不意外呢？因為你每一次都打翻啊。

---

2. take someone's words seriously　把某人的話當一回事

I told you he is bad news, why don't you **take my words seriously.**

我跟你説過不要跟他沾上關係，為什麼你不聽我的話。

---

3. all year round　全年、整年

I enjoy eating hot pot **all year round,** even if it is in the middle of summer.

我不管什麼時候都喜歡吃火鍋，就算是夏天。

---

4. out of someone's expectation　在某人的意料之外

I can't believe Howard and Lina actually got married. This is so **out of my expectation.**

我不敢相信哈沃和琳娜真的結婚了，真是超乎我想像。

---

5. what's wrong with you　你到底是哪根筋不對

Why do you keep interrupting me, **what's wrong with you**!

為什麼你一直打斷我，你到底想怎樣！

6. **live in la-la land** 搞不清楚狀況，不知道在想什麼

The more I get to know her the more I think she **lives in la-la land.**

當我越了解她我越覺得她怪怪的。

----

7. **mad at someone** 生某人的氣

I hope you are not **mad at me**, I moved your stuff before I had a chance to ask you.

希望你不會生我的氣，我沒問過你就把你的東西移開。

----

8. **an easy fix** 很容易解決

Just log into your account and change the data manually. This is **an easy fix.**

只要登入你的帳號，手動的去改資料，這樣就可以解決。

Unit 39 出門等好久

 前情提要

Kate 每次出門都需要準備很久，Simon 跟朋友約了六點要在餐廳吃晚餐，他五點就已經到 Kate 家接她了，可是她還沒好。

人物角色

- Simon 男朋友
- Kate 女朋友

情境對話 MP3 39

Simon: Are you nearly ready? We have to be **on our way** in 5 mins **in order to** get there in time.

賽門：你差不多好了嗎？我們五分鐘後一定要出門，不然來不及。

Kate: Almost done, I just need to change my clothes.

凱特：差不多了，我換一下衣服就好了。

Simon: What you are wearing is fine, you look great in that dress.

賽門：你穿這樣很好啊！這件洋裝很適合你。

Kate: But I think it looks a bit too **out there**. Maybe I should just wear something more casual. Just give me a second.

凱特：可是我覺得太招搖了，我看我還是穿輕鬆一點，等我一下就好。

Simon: Honestly, I think what you are wearing is perfectly fine and we need to **get going** because we are late every time.

賽門：說真的，你穿這樣很 OK，我們真的要出門了，因為我們每次都遲到。

Kate: Why are you always in such a hurry, just **chill out**. I am pretty myself up so you can **show me off** to your friends. You should be thanking me for **putting in so much effort** to **make you look good!**

凱特：為什麼你每次都那麼急？放輕鬆阿，我精心打扮是要讓你在朋友面前可以炫耀你有這麼正的女友，你應該感謝我這麼用心地讓你有面子！

01 留學生與外派人員

02 上班族

03 異國情侶

04 背包客和觀光客

 慣用語

1. on someone's way 出門了

She just sent me a message to say she is **on her way.**

她剛傳簡訊過來說她出門了。

---

2. in order to 為了、才可以

In order to get here in time, I had to take a taxi because my car is in repair right now.

為了要準時到這裡，我還搭計程車過來，因為我的車在維修。

---

3. out there 招搖

Bright pink and yellow stripes? If it is not **out there** I don't know what is.

螢光粉紅還有黃色的橫條，如果這不算招搖什麼才算呢？

---

4. get going 要走了

Thanks for a nice evening, but I'd better **get going** because it is getting late.

謝謝你的美好夜晚，可是我可能要先走了，時間有點晚。

---

5. chill out 放鬆一點

All I want to do after work is to sit down and **chill out.**

下班之後我只想坐下來放鬆。

---

6. show something/ someone off 炫耀

We all know Mr. Foster just bought a new sports car, he

couldn't stop **showing it off.**

我們都知道佛斯特先生最近買了一台新的跑車，因為他不停地炫耀。

----

7. **put in effort** 用心、努力

I **put in so much effort** to organize her birthday party. She better be impressed.

我這麼用心計畫她的生日派對，她千萬不要跟我說她不喜歡。

----

8. **make someone look good** 讓某人有面子、讓某人占優勢

He made such a silly mistake, and that even **makes me look good.**

他犯了這麼大的錯，跟他比起來我還算好。

Unit 40 生活習慣不同

前情提要

Zach 來自紐西蘭,跟台灣的女朋友 Esther 同住一個公寓。Esther 不太能接受為什麼 Zach 晚上不洗澡,一定要睡醒早上才洗澡。Esther 想辦法要跟他溝通。

人物角色

● Zach 男朋友
● Esther 女朋友

情境對話

`MP3 40`

Esther: Why don't you go and have a shower before bed? It will make you feel better.

艾絲特:你要不要睡前洗個澡?這樣你會比較舒服。

Zach: Why? Do I smell? I had show-

札克:為什麼?我很臭

er this morning.

Esther: You know it is not like New Zealand here. It is 35 degrees today and you have **been out all day**. Don't you want to **rinse off** all the dirt and sweat on your body?

Zach: I know **you've got a point there**, but I am ok, it doesn't **bother me**. I will go and have a shower if that bothers you.

Esther: I don't want to be mean, but I will really appreciate that if you do.

Zach: All right, I will do it for you.

Esther: Oh, that's so sweet! Thanks, this **means a lot to me**.

嗎？我今天早上洗過了。

艾絲特：你知道這裡跟紐西蘭不一樣，今天三十五度而且你整天在外面跑。你不想把身上的髒污沖掉嗎？

扎克：我知道你說得有道理，我是覺得還好，我沒很介意，可是如果你介意的話，那我就去洗澡。

艾絲特：我不想要讓你覺得我很機車可是如果你可以去洗澡的話，我會很感謝的。

扎克：好吧，為了你才這樣做。

艾絲特：喔～你真是太貼心了！謝謝，我真的很感動。

 **慣用語**

1. being out all day　整天在外面

I can do with a cold drink right now. I have **been out all day** in the sun.

我真想來杯冰涼飲料，今天在太陽下跑了一整天。

---

2. rinse off　沖掉

This lotion is so greasy, I can't stand it. I have to **rinse it off.**

這個乳液好黏，我受不了了，要沖掉。

---

3. someone has got a point there　某人講得有道理

I really don't want to admit it, but I think my mum **has got a point there**, he is not good for me.

我真的很不想承認，但我想我媽是對的，他真的不是個好男人

---

4. bother someone　讓某人覺得很煩

I am avoiding him because he keeps **bothering me.**

我一直在躲他，因為他一直煩我

---

5. means a lot to someone　對某人來很感動

Thanks for looking after my family. That **means a lot to me.**

謝謝你照顧我的家人，我真的很感動。

---

6. not someone's cup of tea　個人喜好不同

I won't force him to watch a girly movie with me, I know it is

not his cup of tea.

我不會逼他看女生愛看的電影，我知道他並不喜歡。

---

7. **see eye to eye**　很有默契、品味相同

I don't need to say a lot of things to him. We just seems to **see eye to eye.**

很多事情我不用先跟他說，我們好像默契很好。

---

8. **do someone's best**　盡力了

I think things did not turn out the way we wanted, but honestly I have **done my best.**

我知道事情的發展不如我們預期的，可是我真的盡力了。

Unit 41 去誰家過節

前情提要

Denise 跟 Adrian 交往了一年多。因為已經打算結婚 Adrian 希望 Denise 今年可以跟他一起回美國過聖誕順便見家人。

人物角色

- Denise 女朋友
- Adrian 男朋友

情境對話 `MP3 41`

Adrian: I think you should come with me to the US this Xmas, I think **it's about time** for you to meet them. You know my mam is your **biggest fan,** they are **dying to** meet you in person.

安德恩：我覺得你今年聖誕應該跟我一起回美國，也差不多要見見我的家人吧！你知道我媽最愛你了，他超想見你本人的！

Denise: I don't know honey, you know Xmas matter to my parents being Catholic. We always go to the church together which is our **family tradition**. Why don't you join us since you are going to be **part of the family** soon. We can go visit them later this year.

Adrian: it wouldn't have been the same. I really miss being home for Xmas.

Denise: I know your parents would love to have us there for Xmas, but the plane tickets are too costly during **peak season.** Maybe we can **plan ahead** and save up for the tickets from now on. Then we should have enough to visit them next Xmas.

狄尼絲：我懂，親愛的⋯你知道我爸媽是天主教徒，聖誕節對他們很重要。我們會一起去教堂，這是我家的傳統。不如你跟我們一起來吧，反正你也快成為我們家的一員了。我們之後可以再找個時間去看他們。

安德恩：可是那不一樣，我真的很懷念回家過聖誕的感覺。

狄尼絲：我知道你爸媽也很想跟我們一起過聖誕，旺季的機票很貴，不如我們現在開始存機票錢，明年聖誕就夠錢去看他們了吧！

 **慣用語**

1. it's about time　早就應該，也是時候

I think **it's about time** for us to set up another meeting to see where we at.

也是時候再開個會看一下大家的進度吧！

---

2. biggest fan　最喜歡

You know I am your **biggest fan**. I will support you regardless.

你知道我欣賞你了，無論如何我都會支持你。

---

3. dying to do something　迫不及待想做某事

I am **dying to** find out whether I get the job or not.

我好想知道到底那份工作有沒有要請我。

---

4. family tradition　家族傳統

Being away for Chinese New Year is kind of against my **family tradition**.

過年不回家這種事，我家不太能接受。

---

5. part of the family　家庭成員

My puppet dog is considered as **part of the family**, too.

我家的小狗也是我家的一員。

---

6. it wouldn't have been the same　可是那不一樣

It wouldn't have been the same without you there.

如果你不去那就不一樣了!

---

7. **peak season** 旺季

I can't afford to go overseas during **peak season**.

我負擔不起忘記去旅行的費用。

---

8. **plan ahead** 提早準備

It is very hard for me to get time off work, we need to **plan ahead** if we wanted to go travel.

我很難請假,所以如果要去旅遊我們要提早計畫。

Memo

Unit 42 不喜歡對方父母

前情提要

Lindsay 一直以來都與 Aiden 的媽媽處得不好，這天 Aiden 媽媽又講了一些 Lindsay 不中聽的話。 Lindsay 在跟 Aiden 抱怨。

人物角色

- Aiden 男朋友
- Lindsay 女朋友

情境對話 MP3 42

Lindsay: Do you know what your mum said to me? She told me I have been ungracious. I think she is really rude.

琳希：你知道你媽跟我說什麼嗎？她說我沒規矩，我覺得她才沒禮貌！

Aiden: I am sorry if she offended

伊登：真的很對不起，如

you, I am sure she **means well.** You just **took it the wrong way.**

果她得罪你，你知道她是好意，應該是你誤會她了！

Lindsay: Are you **taking her side**? You didn't even ask me what happened and you started to defend her.

琳希：你的意思是你站在她那邊囉？你連問都沒問發生什麼事就開始幫她説話！

Aiden: No, no, no... I am sorry, please tell me what happen exactly.

伊登：沒有沒有！對不起，那可以跟我説妳到底發生什麼事嗎？

Lindsay: You always **jump into conclusions** before you **hear me out**, **why should I bother** justifying for myself. Go home and being a **mummy's boy,**

琳希：你總是不先聽我説就下結論，為什麼我還要費力氣解釋給你聽。回家當你的媽寶吧！

Aiden: You know it is hard to be **stuck in the middle**. I will make sure my mum wouldn't say anything more to upset you.

伊登：你知道卡在你們中間有多痛苦，我保證我媽不會再説那種得罪你的話了！

慣用語

1. mean well　好意

I know you **mean well**, but you really have to think twice before you speak.

我知道你是好意，可是你講話前真的要三思再開口。

---

2. take it the wrong way　誤會

It is very hard not to **take it the wrong way**, what you just said is really offensive.

你剛講的話真的很容易得罪人，讓人不誤會你也難

---

3. take someone's side　站在某人的那邊

I really need you to back me up, are you going to **take my side**?

我真的很需要你的支持，你會站在我這邊嗎？

---

4. jump into conclusions　衝動，沒考慮清楚就下決定

Don't just **jump into conclusions**. You always make mistakes like that.

不要沒考慮清楚就下決定，你每次都是這樣衝動。

---

5. hear someone out　聽某人說

I know everyone thinks it is her fault, but I think we need to **hear her out**. Maybe she has been mistaken.

我知道每個人都覺得是她的錯，可是我覺得應該聽聽她怎麼說，可能

我們都誤會了。

---

6. **why should someone bother...** 為何某人還要費力氣去…

Why should I bother to prove myself, he already told me I am not going to make it.

為什麼我還要費力氣去證明我自己，他都已經跟我說我不會成功了。

---

7. **mummy's boy** 媽寶

Jarrod is such a **mummy's boy**. He couldn't make any decision without his mom's opinions.

傑若真是個媽寶，沒問過他媽他不敢下決定。

---

8. **stuck in the middle** 夾在中間

I hate being **stuck in the middle** between Jenny and Yvonne whenever they got into an argument.

珍妮和伊方吵架時我最討厭被夾在中間了！

Unit 43 不適當的穿著

前情提要

Declan 的父母來訪,他要介紹他的女友 Louise 給他的父母認識。Louise 平常喜歡穿得性感一點,她不覺得這樣見家長有什麼不妥。

人物角色

- Declan 男朋友
- Louise 女朋友

情境對話　　　　MP3 43

Declan: Honey, I really love your beautiful legs, but I don't know whether my parents are going to appreciate the same. Why don't you **put on** that nice dress you wore the other day?

戴克林:親愛的,我真的很愛你的美腿,可是我不確定我爸媽會欣賞。為什麼不穿你那天穿的那件美美的洋裝呢?

Louise: It is **nerve-wracking** enough for me to meet your parents **for the first time**, I do want to **make an impression**, but I also want them to **like me for me.**

Declan: I know what you mean, but you got to understand they are the conservative kind. They are the firm believers of traditional values. Please **take my advice,** they are not **a big fan of** hot pants. You can still wear something else and be you.

Louise: Well, if you say so. I do like that dress, too. Alright, I will **get changed** then.

露易絲：第一次見你爸媽已經夠我緊張了，我想製造好印象，可是我不想太做作。

戴克林：我懂你的意思，可是你要了解我爸媽是很保守的那種，他們相信傳統的價值觀，聽我的建議他們真的不太喜歡超短褲。你可以穿不同的衣服可是還是你啊！

露易絲：好吧！既然你這麼說，我也很愛那件洋裝。那我去換衣服了。

🗨 慣用語

1. **put on** 穿上

Why don't you **put on** something nice, since we are going to the theater tonight.

既然我們今天晚上要去劇場，不如好好打扮一下。

---

2. **nerve-wracking** 緊張

It is very **nerve-wracking** to know I will be interviewed by the CEO of the company.

知道公司的執行長會親自面試我，實在很讓人緊張。

---

3. **for the first time** 第一次

I will be stepping in for my manager, while he is on holiday **for the first time.**

這是我第一次幫我的經理代理職務，因為他要去休假。

---

4. **make an impression** 製造好印象

She is the girl of my dreams, I really want to **make a good impression.**

她是我的夢中情人，我真的很想留下一個好印象。

---

5. **like someone for someone** 真心的喜歡某人

I deliberately not put on any makeup because I want him to **like me for me.**

跟他出去我故意不化妝，因為我想要他喜歡真正的我。

6. take someone's advice　聽我的建議

Take my advice and put on a tie, Mrs. Mulder prefers the formal look.

跟你說最好打條領帶去，穆德太太喜歡比較正式的打扮。

---

7. a big fan of　喜歡

I am not **a big fan of** red wine. I found it too strong.

我不太喜歡紅酒，我覺得味道太強烈。

---

8. get changed　換衣服

Wearing the tight jeans is killing me. I am going to **get changed.**

穿著緊身牛仔褲好不舒服，我要去換衣服了。

Unit 44 奇怪的簡訊

🧠 前情提要

最近 Owen 常常偷偷的躲起來講電話，也一直在傳訊息，每次 Nicole 問起他就說是同事有事要他幫忙。有 Owen 的朋友偷偷跟 Nicole 講，叫她要注意 Owen。這天已經很晚了，Owen 的手機又有訊息進來，Nicole 終於受不了了，搶他的手機來看，是一個叫 Lucy 跟 Owen 說睡不著，很想他。

👤 人物角色

● Nicole 正牌女友
● Owen 男友
● Lucy 有可能是小三

👄 情境對話 ⸺⸺⸺⸺ MP3 44

Nicole: Who the hell is Lucy, are you **cheating on me**? How can you do

妮可：這個露西是哪裡冒出來的？你有小三是不

this to me! I am nothing but nice to you.

是？你怎麼可以這樣對我呢？我對你不好嗎！

Owen: Listen to me honey, I can explain. She is just a friend. It is not what it looks like.

歐文：親愛的聽我説，我可以解釋，她只是個朋友，不是你想的這樣。

Nicole: What does it look like then? If you weren't **involved with her,** why did she text you this late at night?

妮可：那不然是怎樣？如果你沒跟她有一腿，那她幹嘛這麼晚傳簡訊給你？

Owen: She just moved here and I was just helping her to **settle in.** Maybe she just **got the wrong idea** about me.

歐文：她只是剛搬來，我幫忙她安頓下來而已。可能她有點會錯意了。

Nicole: What a liar, I know you are **leading her on**. You even **went out of your way** to go and see her yesterday. I trusted you **with all my heart**, but you have **gone too far** this time.

妮可：別騙了！我知道你也對她放電，你昨天還特別去找她。我以前全心全意地相信你，可是這次你真的太過分了！

 **慣用語**

1. cheating on someone　背著某人有外遇

I just saw Phil kiss that girl, I can't believe he is **cheating on Maddie**.

我剛看到菲爾親那個女孩，我不敢相信他背著蔓蒂在外亂來。

---

2. involved with someone　跟某人有關係、在交往

I suspect Donald is **involved with Nicky**, but they didn't tell anyone.

我懷疑唐諾應該是跟妮琪在交往，可是他們什麼都沒說。

---

3. settle in　安頓下來

I think it will take me a while to **settle in.**

我覺得我需要一段時間才會安頓下來

---

4. get the wrong idea　會錯意

I really wish he didn't **get the wrong idea**. All I want is to be friends with him.

我希望他不要會錯意，我真的只想跟他當朋友。

---

5. leading someone on　搞曖昧

Oliver is **leading her on** deliberately. He just has no shame.

奧利佛是故意要對她放電的，他真是不要臉。

---

6. go out of someone's way　特別、專程

Thank you for **going out of your way** to come and visit me, I know you are very busy.

謝謝你專程來看我，我知道你很忙。

---

7. **with all my heart**　全心全意

I will stand by you **with all my heart.** All I want is for you to be happy.

無論如何我都會支持你，我只是想要你快樂。

---

8. **gone too far**　太過分了、太超過了

This has **gone too far.** I don't think there is anything I can do to fix this.

這個情況已經失控了，我可能沒辦法處理。

193

Unit 45 有人來搭訕

前情提要

Kimmy 在位置上等男朋友去買飲料回來，突然間有個人來搭訕，她只想叫他不要煩她。

👤 人物角色

- **Carl** 前來搭訕的人
- **Kimmy** 在等男友回來的小姐

👄 情境對話 　　　　　　　　　MP3 45

Carl: Hey Sexy, can I **buy you a drink**?

卡爾：美女，可以請你喝杯酒嗎？

Kimmy: I am sorry I am **with somebody** here. Maybe not a good idea, but thanks for the offer.

琪咪：不好意思我有人陪了，這樣不太好，還是謝謝你的好意。

Carl: Well, he is one lucky guy, I hope he knows it, but what is he doing leaving a beautiful girl like you here alone.

Kimmy: Thanks for your concern but it is **none of your business.** He is getting me a drink now, he will be right back. Take my advice, you should leave now. He doesn't appreciate when people **step into** his territory.

Carl: Well, if you **change your mind**, I would be at the bar. You know where to find me.

Kimmy: Thanks but no thanks. **You are really not my type**, just **leave me alone**.

卡爾：嗯，我希望他知道他真的是個幸運兒！可是他為什麼把你這樣的美女一個人留在這裡？

琪咪：謝謝你的關心，可是這不甘你的事，他是去幫我買飲料，馬上就回來，你最好現在就離開。聽我的話，他最討厭別人侵犯到他的地盤。

卡爾：好吧！如果你改變主意的話，我就在吧檯，你找的到我的！

琪咪：謝謝，但是真的不用！你不是我的菜，拜託你離開。

01 留學生與外派人員

02 上班族

03 異國情侶

04 背包客和觀光客

 慣用語

1. buy someone a drink　請某人喝杯飲料

I would like to **buy a drink** for the pretty girl sitting by the window.

我想請那個坐在窗邊的美女喝杯酒。

2. with somebody　有人陪

Kenny wanted to ask that lady out, but he just found out she is always **with somebody.**

肯尼想要約那個女生出去，可是才發現她已經有男友了。

3. thanks for your concern　謝謝你的關心

Thanks for your concern, I know this is going to be difficult but I decided to go ahead anyway.

謝謝你的關心，我知道這會很困難可是我還是決定要做。

4. none of your business　不干你的事

I will appreciate you stay out of this, because this is **none of your business.**

我勸你不要插手，因為不甘你的事。

5. step into　踏入、闖入

Have you been to the new restaurant on the corner? It is like you accidently **stepped into** the 80's, the décor is so dated.

你有去過轉角那間新餐廳嗎？好像回到八零年代，裝修好俗氣喔。

6. change someone's mind　改變主意

Taryn **changed her mind**, and she decides to go to college next year.

泰倫改變她的想法了，她決定明年要去念大學。

---

7. someone is not my type　某人不是我的菜

I know Derek is popular, but **he really is not my type.**

我知道德瑞克很受歡迎，可是他真的不是我的菜。

---

8. leave someone alone　不要煩某人

John is in a terrible mood at the moment. Let's just **leave him alone** for now.

約翰現在心情很差，我們最好不要煩他。

01 留學生與外派人員

02 上班族

03 異國情侶

04 背包客和觀光客

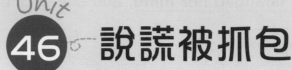

冤家英語

Unit 46 說謊被抓包

前情提要

Teresa 發現男友騙她，對此感到非常生氣。

人物角色

- Teresa 女朋友
- Logan 男朋友
- Mary Teresa 好朋友

情境對話　　　　MP3 46

Teresa: Where are you now Logan?

泰瑞莎：羅根，你在哪裡？

Logan: I am with a client at the moment, I can't really talk, can I call you back **in a second**?

羅根：我跟客戶在一起，現在不方便說話，等一下再回你電話好嗎？

Teresa: Let me ask you, are you at the little Italy restaurant right now?

泰瑞莎：我問你，你現在是不是在小義大利餐廳？

Logan: Well... hmmm... No, I am **out of town** on a business trip as I told you.

羅根：嗯，那個，沒有啊！我不是跟你説我到外地去出差嗎？

Teresa: Stop telling me lies! Mary just saw you there with a girl, you were **hand in hand** with her. You are a liar! We are done!

泰瑞莎：別騙了！瑪莉剛才看到你跟一個女的，你還跟她手牽手，你這個騙子，我們玩完了！

Logan: Please don't be mad, I can explain. She is just **a fling**, I am **not into her, you are the one** Theresa!

羅根：拜託你不要生氣，聽我解釋，我跟她只不過是玩玩而已，我根本對她沒意思，泰瑞莎，你才是我的唯一！

Teresa: You know what, I thought we had a future together, but you just **threw it away.**

泰瑞莎：算了，我曾經以為我們會有未來，可是你一手把它摧毀了。

Logan: I am so sorry I **stuff up**. Please give me another chance.

羅根：我真的很抱歉，我搞砸了！再給我一次機會好不好？

慣用語

1. **In a second**　等一下、稍等

Just leave those reports on the table. I will go through them **in a second.**

先把那些報表放桌上，我等一下看。

---

2. **out of town**　不在居住的城市、到外地

I can't get his signature at the moment because he is **out of town**.

我現在沒辦法找他簽名，因為他不在。

---

3. **hand in hand**　手牽手

They look so sweet **hand in hand** with each other.

他們手牽手的樣子看起來好甜蜜。

---

4. **a fling**　玩玩的、不是認真的

It is just **a fling** with Courtney. There is no future for us.

我跟康妮只是玩玩而已，不可能有未來的。

---

5. **not into someone**　不在乎某人、不願意對某人花心思

To be honest, I think he is **not into you**; otherwise, he would be here by now.

說真的我覺得他沒那麼在乎你，不然他老早就來了。

---

6. **someone is the one**　某人是唯一

From the first moment we met, I knew **she is the one.**

從我們第一次見面的那一刻起，我就知道她是我的真命天女了。

---

7. throw away　丟棄、摧毀

I can't believe he decided to **throw away** his future with her.

我不敢相信他決定放棄跟她一起的未來。

---

8. stuff up　搞砸了

Rita is going to be so mad once she finds out I **stuff up** the booking for dinner.

等瑞塔發現我晚餐的訂位都沒弄好的時候，她一定會發火。

Memo

冤家英語

討厭你的豬朋狗友

 前情提要

　　Stacey 很不喜歡 Corey 的好友 Patrick，因為 Patrick 常常做些蠢事，他更喜歡半夜找 Corey 去喝酒，這點讓 Stacey 很受不了。這天 Patrick 又打電話來找 Corey。

 人物角色

- Stacey 女朋友
- Corey 男朋友
- Patrick Corey 的好朋友
- Cindy Patrick 的前女友

 **情境對話** MP3 47

Stacey: Are you **going out with** Patrick again? It is almost midnight. What are you guys up to going out so late?

史黛西：你又要跟派崔克出去了嗎？都快要十二點了，你們這麼晚出去到底

He is a nut job!

都在幹嘛？他真是瘋的？！

Corey: Honey, you know he just **broke up with** Cindy. He is miserable and doesn't want to be alone. He just couldn't **move on.**

克林：親愛的，你知道他剛跟辛蒂分手，他很可憐，也不想一個人獨處，他只是還沒有走出來。

Stacey: I think Cindy broke up with him **for a reason**, I would have done the same if I was her. He is just **not boyfriend material**.

史黛西：我覺得辛蒂會跟他分手是有她的理由的，要是我我也會這麼做，他真的不適合當男朋友。

Corey: Come on, Stacey, don't talk about him that way.

克林：拜託，你不要這樣說他嘛！

Stacey: Honestly, he is just having a **bad influence** on you. I really don't know what you **see in him.**

史黛西：說真的，他真的是個豬朋狗友，我真不知道你到底欣賞他什麼。

Corey: I know you are not a big fan of him, but he has always **been there for me**, I just can't leave him like this.

克林：我知道你不喜歡他，史黛西，可是他一直都在我身邊，我不能就這樣把他丟著。

 慣用語

1. going out with　跟某人一起出去、約會、交往

Do you know Cecilia is **going out with** Toby? I didn't see this coming.

你知道西西莉亞在跟托比交往嗎？我好意外喔！

---

2. break up with　與某人分手

Brad **broke up with** Gloria last week; therefore, they are not coming to the trip with us.

布萊德跟葛洛莉雅上星期分手了，所以他們就不跟我們去旅行了。

---

3. move on　從困境中走出來、繼續進行

I still couldn't come to terms with what happened to her, but I know I need to **move on.**

我還是不太能接受她出了這麼大的事，可是我知道我需要走出來。

---

4. for a reason　事出必有因

I believe Michelle met Jason **for a reason.** They really suit each other.

我覺得蜜雪兒遇見傑森是注定的，他們很適合對方。

---

5. not something material　不適合做某事

Brett is totally **not husband material**, he just couldn't be tighten down by just one woman.

布瑞真的不適合當老公，因為他不會為了一棵樹而放棄整片森林。

6. **bad influence**　豬朋狗友、壞影響

Derek is such a **bad influence**, I really don't want you to spend too much time with him.

德瑞克是個豬朋狗友，我真的不希望你太常跟他在一起。

---

7. **see in someone**　你欣賞他哪一點

I always wonder what you **see in Joslyn**. She seems really bossy to me.

我總是在想你到底欣賞裘瑟琳什麼？我覺得她很愛發號施令埃。

---

8. **be there for someone**　陪在某人身邊、支持某人

Thank you for always **being there for me**, I think I am very lucky to have a friend like you.

謝謝你一直都在我身邊，我真的很幸運有你這樣的朋友。

Unit 48 吵架過後

 前情提要

Matthew 跟 Maddison 交往了好一陣子，可是大吵小吵不斷。這天又為了生活瑣事吵了一架，Matthew 看得出 Maddison 已經快要放棄了，所以他決定先跟 Maddison 道歉，看能不能挽回。

人物角色

- **Matthew** 男朋友
- **Maddison** 女朋友

情境對話　MP3 48

Matthew: I am sorry, I was very mean and aggressive. I didn't meant to hurt you. Let's just **put this behind us**, and **start over** again. I know you

馬修：很抱歉，我剛很刻薄又很兇，我不是故意要讓你傷心。我們就當沒發生過，重新開始好不好？

got a point, and I will try to **take it in**.

我知道你説得有道理，我會盡量改。

Maddison: You say the same thing every time we fight, if you want me to believe in you this time, you really need to **play your cards right**. My patience is **running thin** here.

麥德森：每次我們吵架你都這樣説，如果你還要我相信你的話你最好認真的好好表現。我對你真的沒什麼耐性了！

Matthew: it takes time Maddie, you can't expect me to chango overnight. But I promise I will **give it my best shot**.

馬修：這是要花一點時間的，麥蒂，你不能要求我馬上就改掉，我可以答應你我一定會盡力去做。

Maddison: I hope you really **mean it** this time. I do want us to have a future together.

麥德森：我希望你這次是説真的，我真的希望我們能一起走下去。

Matthew: I am sure as long as we **stick together** we would make this work.

馬修：只要我們兩個人一條心，一定可以的！

 慣用語

1. put this behind us　不要再回想了、當這回事沒發生過

I wish we could **put this behind us**. I really don't want to talk about this again.

我希望我們可以放下這件事，因為我不想再提起了。

---

2. start over　重新開始

I made so many mistakes with my ex. I just want to **start over** with someone fresh.

在我的上一段感情中我做了很多錯誤的決定，我現在只想重新開始跟一個新的人交往。

---

3. take it in　聽進去

I know there is a lot of information here, but try to **take it in** as much as you can.

我知道這裡涵蓋了很多資訊，你就盡量可以記得多少是多少。

---

4. play your cards right　好好表現

This is could go either way. You'd better **play your cards right**.

這件事可好好壞，要看你怎麼表現。

---

5. running thin　快要沒了

I could tell his tolerance was **running very thin,** he was about to blow up.

我看得出他的耐性快磨光了，他就要發火了！

6. give it my best shot 盡力

Thanks for giving me this opportunity. I can promise you I will **give it my best shot.**

謝謝你給我這個機會，我可以保證我一定會盡力去做。

---

7. mean it 認真的

I really **mean it**. You got so much potential.

我是說真的，你真的很有潛力。

---

8. stick together 一起撐下去

I know we are in trouble now, and I really need us to **stick together.**

我知道我們現在的情況不好，可是我真的需要我們同心協力。

冤家英語

Unit 49 金錢觀念不同

前情提要

Joanna 跟 Lachlan 有考慮要結婚，可是 Joanna 一直很擔心 Lachlan 的財務會調不過來，她想跟他好好談一談。

人物角色

- ◉ Joanna 女朋友
- ◉ Lachlan 男朋友

情境對話 `MP3 49`

Joanna: I know you **prefer to** put everything on the credit card and only **make the minimum payment** each month, but if you **do the math**, we are actually paying 3 times as much by the time we made the final repay-

喬安娜：我知道你情願把所有的東西都用信用卡付款每個月只繳最低應繳，可是如果你仔細算一下，當我們終於把欠款繳清時，我們其實付了三倍的

210

ment. I mean, **what's the point!** Can't we just **pay it off** every month? It is not like we **can't afford it.**

Lachlan: Well, I suppose we can do that, but you do realize that way it would **take a toll on** our cash flow.

Joanna: I understand, but I feel really uncomfortable knowing we owe so much and we will be spending next 3 years paying them off. I think we should relook our **spending habit.**

錢。我的意思是，這有比較好嗎？為什麼我們不每個月就把它解決，我們又不是付不出來。

洛克林：嗯，我想應該可以吧！可是你要了解這樣會影響我們的現金流。

喬安娜：我懂，只是我只要想到我們欠那麼多錢，接下來還要花二年才還得完，就真的覺得很不舒服。我覺得我們應該重新審視我們的消費模式。

01 留學生與外派人員

02 上班族

03 異國情侶

04 背包客和觀光客

 慣用語

1. Prefer to　情願、比較喜歡

Compared with a French cuisine, I think I much **prefer to** eat Italian food.

跟法國菜比起來，我比較喜歡吃義大利菜。

---

2. make the payment　付款

Frank would be unable to **make those payments** if he lost his job.

法蘭克如果失去他的工作，他就付不出那些錢了。

---

3. do the math　算算看

Why don't you **do the math**, I don't think we have much money to spare each month.

為什麼你不算算看，我們每個月的錢都所剩無幾。

---

4. what's the point　這又何苦呢？

He is never going to treat you right, **what's the point**? Why don't you just let go.

他真的不會真心對你好，你又是何苦呢？為什麼不放手。

---

5. pay something off　付清

I am so excited, I am 2 payments away from completely **paying my car off.**

我好興奮，我在兩期就可以把車貸付清了！

6. can't afford something　負擔不起某物

If you had to borrow from others, then you **couldn't afford it.**

如果你需要借錢買某樣東西，那就代表你負擔不起那樣東西。

---

7. take a/its toll on something　影響某事

This financial trouble we are in is **taking its toll on** our relationship.

我們的財務問題已經開始影響我們的關係了。

---

8. spending habit　消費模式

I think buying latest phone each month is definitely not a healthy **spending habit.**

我認為每個月都換新手機絕對不是一種好的消費模式。

01 留學生與外派人員

02 上班族

03 美國情侶

04 背包客和觀光客

Unit 50 家事的分配

🗨 前情提要

　　Kevin 是個傳統的男生，這天 Iris 與 Kevin 剛好在聊有關家事應該是誰的責任，Iris 想趁這個機會把話說清楚，讓 Kevin 多分擔一點家事。

👤 人物角色

- Iris 女朋友
- Kevin 男朋友

👄 情境對話　　　　MP3 50

Iris: I know you **work your butt off** at work, but so do I. I really think the house chores should be **divided evenly** between us two.

艾莉絲：我了解你工作一整天很辛苦，可是我不是嗎？我真的覺得家事應該要兩個人分工合作。

Kevin: I think it is more a woman's job, **you are a natural**! I just can't do it as well as you do.

Iris: Well, You might think being a woman I **was born to** do the house work and **keeping it in order**, but honestly, that is very last generation.

Kevin: Alright, I will try to **make more effort.** How about you cook dinner on Monday and Thursday. Then I am happy to do it for Tuesday and Friday. Then we can eat out on Wednesday and the weekends, what do you think?

Iris: Sounds fair. I can **sit back and relax** a little. What do you want to do with laundry then?

凱文：我覺得家事比較像是女人的工作，你比較在行，說真的我做的又沒有你好。

艾莉絲：你可能覺得女人就應該負責家庭大小事，可是老實說那真的是上個世代的事了。

凱文：好啦，我會努力。如果你負責星期一、四煮晚餐的話，那我願意負責星期二、五。星期三和六日我們就出去吃吧，這樣也不用洗碗。這樣好不好？

艾莉絲：聽起來蠻公平的，這樣我就可以坐下來放鬆了，那洗衣服的工作怎麼分配？

慣用語

1. work someone's butt off 辛苦工作

Seth has been **working his butt off** lately. I think his girl is feeling a bit neglected.

賽斯最近日以繼夜的工作，我覺得他的女朋友可能覺得被忽略了。

---

2. divide evenly 平均分配

It is hard to **divide the tasks evenly**. Someone is always going to complain.

要平均分配工作實在很難，總是會有人抱怨不公平。

---

3. someone is a natural 天生好手

Have you seen the way Harry moves, **he is a natural** on the dance floor!

你有看過哈利跳舞嗎？他真的是天生好手！

---

4. be born to 注定要

He is always looking for new challenges. He **was definitely born to** be a risk taker.

他總是在找新的挑戰，他注定是要來冒險的！

---

5. keep something in order 管理、持家

I have to **keep the company in order** when my boss is away.

我老闆不在的時候我要負責管理公司。

6. **make an/more effort**　**再努力一點**

How can you expect me to **make more effort,** I already gave everything!

你怎麼能再教我要努力一點，我已經盡力了!

---

7. **sounds fair**　**聽起來很公平**

I think it **sounds fair** to me. I would not like to do this alone.

聽起來很公平因為我也不想自己做。

---

8. **sit back and relax**　**坐下來放鬆**

It is 9 pm and the housework is done, I can finally **sit back and relax.**

九點了，家事也做完了，我終於可以坐下來放鬆。

Unit 51 我們分手吧

🗨 前情提要

Olivia 一直都很自以為是，Max 跟他交往了幾個月之後覺得受不了了，決定跟 Olivia 提分手。

👤 人物角色

● Max 男朋友
● Olivia 女朋友

👄 情境對話 ⸺ MP3 51

Max: This is **driving me insane**! We are **flighting constantly over** the smallest thing. I just can't take it anymore.

麥斯：我快瘋了！我們不斷地為了芝麻小事吵架，我真的受不了了！

Olivia: What do you want to do then?

奧莉維亞：那你想怎樣？

Max: I don't think we should see each other anymore. We can't even talk to each other properly without **getting into a fight**. I am tired of doing this. Being in a relationship is not **supposed to be** so draining.

Olivia: What can I say, I've done the best I could and I felt you never appreciate my effort at all. I want to **give it another shot** but if that is not what you **have in mind,** I won't force you to do something that you don't what to.

Max: This is hard for me, too. Let's just take a break from each other, and **see where it takes us** maybe some space will **do us good.**

麥斯：我覺得我們應該分開一陣子，我們只要開口講話就一定會吵起來，我真的厭倦這種生活了，談感情不應該是這樣痛苦。

奧莉維亞：我還能説什麼，我也是盡力了，我覺得你從來不感激我的付出。我是還想再試試看，看我們的關係會不會好轉。可是如果你並不這麼打算的話，我也不會逼你做你不想做的事。

麥斯：我也很難受，我看我們還是暫時不要聯絡，看情況再説。也許留點空間對我們兩個都好。

 慣用語

1. driving someone insane　讓某人發瘋

He keeps playing heavy metal music, this is **driving me insane**!

我快發瘋了，他不停地放重金屬樂！

---

2. fight over　爭奪、為了某事吵架

Can you two stop yelling at each other please? He is just not worth **fighting over** for!

你們兩個可不可以不要吵了！他根本就不值得你們倆為他吵架。

---

3. get into a fight　吵起來

I don't know what happened to them, and suddenly they **got into a fight**.

我不知道他們是怎麼了，突然間兩個就吵起來了。

---

4. suppose to be　應該是

She was **supposed to be** the one. I hate myself for letting her slipped away.

其實本來應該要娶她的，我真是恨我自己讓她溜走了。

---

5. give it another shot　再試一次

I don't know how I can get it wrong. I will definitely **give it another shot**.

我不知道為什麼我會做錯，我一定會再試一次。

6. have in mind 有什麼主意、有什麼想法

What do you **have in mind** for dinner? How does Indian sound?

你晚餐想吃什麼？吃印度菜怎麼樣？

---

7. see where it takes someone 看看結果如何、隨緣

I would like a fresh start with Felix and **see where it takes us.**

我想跟菲力士重新開始，看看會不會有結果。

---

8. do someone good 對某人有幫助、使某人學到教訓

He is suspended from driving for 3 months. I think it would **do him good**.

他被吊銷執照三個月，這應該會讓他好好反省。

篇章回顧

 精選慣用語

1. an easy fix 很容易解決

Just log into your account and change the data manually. This is **an easy fix**.

只要登入你的帳號,手動的去改資料,這樣就可以解決。

----

2. someone has got a point there 某人講得有道理

I really don't want to admit it, but I think my mum **has got a point there**, he is not good for me.

----

3. dying to do something 迫不及待想做某事

I am **dying to** find out whether I get the job or not.

我好想知道到底那份工作有沒有要請我。

----

4. stuck in the middle 夾在中間

I hate being **stuck in the middle** between Jenny and Yvonne whenever they got into an argument.

珍妮和伊方吵架時我最討厭被夾在中間了!

5. nerve-wracking 緊張

It is very **nerve-wracking** to know I will be interviewed by the CEO of the company.

知道公司的執行長會親自面試我，實在很讓人緊張。

---

6. not into someone 不在乎某人、不願意對某人花心思

To be honest, I think he is **not into you**; otherwise, he would be here by now.

說真的我覺得他沒那麼在乎你，不然他老早就來了。

---

7. not something material 不適合做某事

Brett is totally **not husband material** because he just couldn't be tighten down by just one woman.

布瑞真的不適合當老公，因為他不會為了一棵樹而放棄整片森林。

---

8. play your card right 好好表現

This is could go either way. You better **play your card right.**

這件事可好好壞，要看你怎麼表現。

PART 04
背包客和觀光客

學習進度表

- [ ] 52. 找工作
- [ ] 53. 住宿
- [ ] 54. 沒拿到薪水
- [ ] 55. 被騙
- [ ] 56. 交通安排
- [ ] 57. 車禍保險
- [ ] 58. 租車
- [ ] 59. 分擔油錢
- [ ] 60. 開車被臨檢
- [ ] 61. 看醫生沒有保險
- [ ] 62. 沒趕上飛機
- [ ] 63. 飯店預約被取消
- [ ] 64. 取消訂房
- [ ] 65. 不滿意旅行團的服務
- [ ] 66. 迷路
- [ ] 67. 退換貨
- [ ] 68. 折扣算錯
- [ ] 69. 機場退稅
- [ ] 70. 護照弄丟重新申請

看完的單元也別忘了打勾喔！！

Unit 52 找工作

🧠 前情提要

　　Arthur 剛抵達澳洲準備展開他一年的打工度假計畫,他在臉書的社團上發現有到農場的工作機會,可是地點在昆士蘭的小鎮,他想打電話過去問問細節。

👤 人物角色

- Arthur 背包客
- Bruce 農場主人

👄 情境對話　　　　MP3 52

Bruce: Yes, we are looking for <u>seasonal workers</u> for cucumber picking, have you done any farm work before?

Arthur: <u>I am afraid not,</u> but I am

布魯斯:是的,我們有在徵採小黃瓜的臨時工,你有做過農場的工作嗎?

亞瑟:不好意思沒有,可

very hardworking. I was wondering how much do you pay and whether the **room and board** are included?

Bruce: Well, it is $22 per hour **before tax.** There is a shed on the farm where you can stay for free, but you have to **supply your own** food. How soon can you start?

Arthur: I can start anytime but the problem is, I **don't have a clue** how to get there, I am in Brisbane right now, and I **rely on** public transportation.

Bruce: My suggestion is to **hop on** a greyhound bus to Bundaberg. Give me a call before you arrive, I can pick you up from the terminal.

是我很認真，我想請問時薪是多少？有包吃住嗎？

布魯斯：嗯，扣稅之前是每個小時 22 塊，農場上有一個農舍你要的話可以免費住，可是食物要自己買。你什麼時候可以開始上班？

亞瑟：我隨時都可以開始，可是有一個問題，我不知道要怎麼去那裡，我目前在布里斯本，我只能搭大眾交通工具。

布魯斯：我建議你搭灰狗巴士到邦達堡，你到之前先打電話給我，我到車站去接你。

01 留學生與外派人員

02 上班族

03 異國情侶

04 背包客和觀光客

 慣用語

1. seasonal workers 季節性的工人

I wish I can find something more permanent, I hate being a **seasonal worker.**

我真希望可以找到長久一點的工作，我很討厭當季節性的工人。

2. I am afraid... 恐怕沒有、不好意思

I am afraid that I haven't heard from her for a long time. There is no much I can tell you.

不好意思我很久都沒有她的消息了，沒有什麼可以告訴你的。

3. room and board 食宿

I was told **room and board** are provided for most of the farm jobs.

我聽説大部分農場的工作都有供食宿。

4. before tax 税前

When you say 25 dollars an hour, do you mean **before or after tax?**

你説每小時 25 塊的意思是扣税前還是扣完税後？

5. supply your own 須自己提供

Some hostels expect you to **supply your own** sheets.

有些青年旅館需要自己帶床單。

6. **not have a clue**　不懂、不知道

She **doesn't have a clue** about how to entering the data into the system.

她完全不知道怎樣輸入資料到這個系統裡。

---

7. **rely on**　依靠

I don't wear a watch, I **rely** solely **on** the phone to tell the time.

我不帶錶的，我完全是靠手機來看時間。

---

8. **hop on**　上車

I can tell you when I will arrive after I **hop on** the train.

等我上車之後我才能告訴你我幾點會到。

Unit 53 住宿

前情提要

Penny 打算在雪梨住三個月,在網路上她看到有雅房出租,她過去看了房子打算搬進去,可是房東說她不歡迎吸菸的人,但 Penny 想再跟房東談談。

人物角色

- Penny 背包客
- Ann 房東

情境對話 `MP3 53`

Penny: I understand you do not welcome a smoker, but I think having a good tenant is **far more** important.

潘妮:我知道你不歡迎抽菸的人,可是我覺得找到一個好的房客才是最重要的。

Ann: I know what you are trying to say, but I really don't want to ruin the new carpet. We only just **had it put in** last year.

Penny: Well, what about if I **keep the smoke away from** the room, I will only smoke when I am outside of the house. Would you consider to **take me in under that condition**?

Ann: I personally would be **happy with it**, but I need to speak to my husband before I can confirm with you.

Penny: I promise you can **count on me**. Plus I am only here for a short time, I would try to **stay out of your way**.

安：我懂你的意思，可是我真的不想把我的新地毯給毀了，我們去年才換過。

潘妮：嗯，那如果我不在房間抽菸呢？我只在房子外面抽，這樣的話你會考慮讓我搬進來嗎？

安：我個人來說是可以接受，可是我還是要問一下我先生，才能跟你確認。

潘妮：我保證我會守信用。何況我只是租短期，我盡量不讓你添麻煩。

慣用語

1. far (more) + adj　很（形容詞）

I think I will go and work Mr. Brennan instead, he pays **far better** than Bruce.

我想我會去班男先生那裡工作，他付的薪水比布魯斯高多了。

---

2. have something put in　安裝某物

We only **had the oven put in** 6 months ago, how can it be broken already?

我們半年前才裝的烤箱，怎麼可能現在就壞掉了？

---

3. Keep something away from　隔離某物

Make sure you **keep your nice jewelleries away from** the kids, they will totally break it.

你千萬不要把你貴重的首飾放在小孩拿的到的地方，他們一定會弄壞。

---

4. take someone in　接納、接受某人

I am so glad they finally decided to **take me in**, I have been house hunting for couple of weeks.

還好他們終於決定要讓我搬進去，我已經找房子找了好幾個禮拜了。

---

5. under the condition　在這個情況或條件下

I was wondering **under what condition** you would allow me take you out?

我在想要怎麼樣你才會答應跟我一起出去？

---

6. happy with it 同意

I have seen the layout of the house. I must say I am **happy with it.**

我看了房子的設計圖，我彎喜歡的。

---

7. count on someone 依賴某人、信任某人

I knew him since we were in high school. I know you can **count on** him.

他從高中我就認識他，我覺得你可以信任他。

---

8. stay out of someone's way 不會使某人添麻煩、不妨礙某人

Thanks for letting me stay, I will try to **stay out of your way.**

謝謝你讓我留下來，我保證不會讓你添麻煩。

01 留學生與外派人員

02 上班族

03 異國情侶

04 背包客和觀光客

Unit 54 沒拿到薪水

前情提要

　　Erin 已經在這間餐廳工作了兩個星期了，可是一直沒拿到薪水，她剛好有個空檔，她決定去問經理。

人物角色

● Erin 員工
● Felice 經理

情境對話　　MP3 54

Erin: Hey Felice, just **a quick word.** I was **under the assumption** the pay day is every Thursday, but I still haven't received my pay **for the past two weeks**.

艾倫：嗨，菲莉絲，我可以跟你談一下嗎？我們不是每個星期四發薪水嗎？可是我到現在都還沒收到前兩個禮拜的薪水。

Felice: Is that right? The pay period is actually every two weeks, but you should have received it **by now.** I am pretty sure I have **signed it off** to payroll last week. Let me check with them for you.

Erin: Thanks for that. I really need the money to pay the bills.

Felice: I just spoke to payroll, apparently your back detail is incorrect, and the payment has been **bounced back**. If you can **head over there** to **fix that up** today, the payment should be in your account by next Thursday.

菲莉絲：是嗎？我們都是兩個星期才發一次，可是你也應該收到了才對。我記得我上星期已經簽出去給薪資部了，我幫你查一下。

艾倫：謝謝你，我真的急著用錢。

菲莉絲：我剛跟薪資部門確認過，你的銀行帳號不正確，所以錢被退回來了。如果你今天過去那裡修改的話，應該下星期四就會進你的帳戶了。

01 留學生與外派人員

02 上班族

03 異國情侶

04 背包客和觀光客

 慣用語

1. **a quick word** 簡單談一下

Let me know if you have a minute. I just want to have **a quick word** with you.

如果你有空讓我知道，我有事想跟你簡單講一下。

---

2. **under the assumption** 以為、假設、認知

For some reason he is **under the assumption** that we are having a training session on Sunday.

不知道為什麼，他一直以為我們星期天有員工訓練。

---

3. **for the past two weeks(time)** 前兩個星期 （時間）

I haven't been feeling well for **the past a few days**.

我已經不舒服好幾天了。

---

4. **by now** 早就應該

Where is our lunch? It should have been here **by now**.

我們的午餐到哪去了？應該早就送來了才對。

---

5. **sign off** 批准

I got my holidays approved. The manager **signed off** this morning.

我的假期申請好了，經理今天早上簽准了！

---

6. **bounce back** 退回

I tried to transfer the money for you, but it got **bounced back** because of the incorrect account number.

我想要轉錢給你可是被退回了，因為帳號不對。

---

7. **head there**　去那裡、過去

I think you should **head over there** as soon as possible. Ms. Fields wants to see you.

我認為你應該趕快過去，菲爾斯小姐有事找你。

---

8. **fix up**　修正、改正

I just realised I made a mistake in that report. I hope I can **fix it up** in time.

我剛發現報告裡面有一個錯誤，希望我米的及修改。

Unit 55 被騙

🌀 前情提要

Freddy 拿到第一次的薪水之後，發現並不是老闆說的 20 塊一個小時，他跑去跟他理論。

👤 人物角色

● **Freddy** 背包客
● **Spencer** 公司老闆

👄 情境對話　　　　　MP3 55

Freddy: Hey Spencer, can I quickly check my last time sheet please? The payment **doesn't seem to add up**.

佛瑞迪：嘿，史班瑟，我可以看一下我上一次的班表嗎？薪水怪怪的。

Spencer: What's wrong with it?

史班瑟：是怎麼樣怪？

Freddy: I **kept a record** for the hours I worked since I started, I should get 1800 dollars this pay, but I only got 1750 dollars. I don't **get it**.

Spencer: The 50 dollars were deducted for the utility bill.

Freddy: You told me I can stay for free. You should have **made it clear** before I started. **I feel like a tool.**

Spencer: Well, **there's no such thing as a free lunch**. **Take it or leave it.**

Freddy: I have no problem paying for what I used, but I do have problems with you not **being upfront with me.**

佛瑞迪：我從第一天就有紀錄上班的時數，我這次的薪水應該是 1800 元，可是怎麼只有 1750 元，我真的不懂。

史班瑟：50 塊是拿來扣水電費的。

佛瑞迪：你說我可以免費住的，我開工前你應該講清楚，我真的覺得被耍了！

史班瑟：嗯，你應該知道天下沒有白吃的午餐，要不要隨便你。

佛瑞迪：要我付水電費是沒問題，可是我的問題是你不坦白跟我說。

 慣用語

1. doesn't add up　不清不楚、對不起來

I don't think Rose is telling the truth, what she said just **doesn't add up.**

我覺得羅莎沒有講實話，她所說的細節都對不起來。

---

2. keep a record　有紀錄

I **kept a record** of all the communication between me and her.

我跟她之間的對話我都有留紀錄。

---

3. get it　了解

I **get it.** You want to spend a romantic evening with Brittney, you don't want us there.

我懂，你是想要跟布蘭妮共享一個浪漫的晚上，你不想要我們打擾。

---

4. make something clear　將某事說清楚

Casey **made it quite clear** that he doesn't want anything to do with her.

凱西說得很清楚，他不想要跟她再有任何關係。

---

5. feel like a fool　覺得被耍了

Nancy stood me up, I just **feel like a fool** now.

南西爽約了，我真的覺得我被耍了！

6. **there's no such thing as a free lunch**　天下沒有白吃的午餐

We both understand **there's no such thing as a free lunch**.
We need to put in effort for it.

我們都知道天下沒有白吃的午餐，我們必須要努力去做。

---

7. **take it or leave it**　要不要是你的事

This is the best thing I can offer right now, **take it or leave it.**

我最多就只能給你這樣，要不要接受是你的選擇。

---

8. **being upfront with someone**　對某人坦白

Please **be upfront with me,** I don't like surprises.

請對我坦白，我個人不喜歡驚喜。

Unit
56 換工作

前情提要

Teddy 這份工作做了一個多月,他覺得老闆不好所以想換工作,有朋友介紹他到別地方去,他打算要跟老闆提離職。

人物角色

- Teddy 背包客
- Parker 老闆

情境對話   MP3 56

Teddy: I don't know **a better way** to **bring this up**. Well, I got a job **line up** in Melbourne and I need to **jump on** the next available flight. So tomorrow would be my last day.

泰迪:我不知道該怎樣開口,嗯,我在墨爾本找到工作,我需要馬上離開,所以明天是我的最後一天。

Parker: You can't do this to me, I need people here, too. You were told that you need to give me at least **two weeks notice** if you are leaving.

派克：你怎麼可以這樣，我這裡也需要人，我跟你說過如果你要走，至少要給我兩個星期的通知。

Teddy: What can I do? They want me to start next week!

泰迪：我能怎麼辦，他們叫我下星期就開工！

Parker: They would have to wait then. I really don't appreciate people **screwing me over.**

派克：你叫他們等，我最不喜歡別人來這套。

Teddy: **What if** I just leave tomorrow?

泰迪：那我如果明天就走怎麼辦？

Parker: You won't see a cent of your pay.

派克：那你就別想拿到薪水。

Teddy: Well, **if that's the case,** I would stay for two weeks. Please take this as my resignation.

泰迪：好吧，如果是這樣的話，我也只能等兩個星期了，那這樣就算你有收到我的離職通知了吧！

01 留學生與外派人員

02 上班族

03 異國情侶

04 背包客和觀光客

 慣用語

1. **a better way** 更好的方式

Tell me if you know **a better way** to do this, I have wasted hours trying to put this together and it is still not done.

如果你知道有更好的方式，可以告訴我。我浪費了很久時間組裝這個東西，可是一直裝不起來。

---

2. **bring something up** 提出某件事

I have been thinking how to **bring this up** to him, I think he would be upset to know I am leaving.

我不知道該怎麼跟他說，如果他知道我要走一定會很生氣。

---

3. **line up** 等待、等著

Forget about him, I am sure there are lots of guys **lining up** to meet you.

忘了他吧！我保證還有很多男生等著認識你。

---

4. **jump on** 搭乘、跳上

I need to **jump on** the next taxi to go to the restaurant. I am so late！

我要趕快搭計程車去餐廳，我已經大遲到了！

---

5. **two weeks notice** 兩個星期的通知、預告

Most of jobs require at least **two weeks notice** for

termination.

大部分的工作都需要給兩個星期的離職通知。

---

6. **screw someone over**　整某人、搞砸某人的計畫

He really **screwed me over.** He left half way without telling anyone.

我被他害死了！他事情做到一半，沒有跟任何人說就消失了。

---

7. **what if...**　那不然…

What if we move everything outside? It would free up some room here, wouldn't it?

那不然我們把東西搬到外面？這樣裡面的空間也會比較大，不是嗎？

---

8. **If that's the case**　如果是這樣的話

If that's the case, I would rather drive than take the public transportation.

如果是這樣的話，我情願開車也不要搭大眾交通工具。

Unit
57 車禍

前情提要

Kirsten 剛到紐西蘭，對於路況不太熟悉。在開車途中不小心跟旁邊的車擦撞，她停下來跟另一個車主理論。

人物角色

- Paul 車主
- Kirsten 觀光客

情境對話　　MP3 57

Paul: What do you think you are doing? You can't just **cut in** like this without indicating! Look you made a dent on the panel. Luckily, no one was injured, but you **freaked me out!**

保羅：你在幹嘛！你不能沒有打燈就切進來！你看板金都凹進去了，還好沒有人受傷，可是我嚇到了！

Kirsten: I didn't see you there. You were at my **blind spot**!

Paul: There is **no excuse**. You should be more careful when you are driving! Focus on the road! I am **in a rush** and the car is still drivable, I think I will just grab your contact detail and let the insurance company **deal with it.**

Kirsten: There is a problem, I am only a traveler here and this car is not insured. I don't know what to do. I think we need to call the police.

Paul: Well, you are **in deep trouble** then. You would have to pay for it with your own money. This would **teach you a lesson.**

Kirsten: it might not be my fault. Let's get the police involved.

柯絲汀：我沒有看到你，你在我的盲點。

保羅：這不是藉口，你開車的時候本來就要小心！注意路況！我現仕趕著要走，車也還能開，不然我就先拿你的聯絡資料再請保險公司處理。

柯絲汀：這有點問題，我只是觀光客，車還沒有保險。我真不知道該怎麼辦，我看還是叫警察吧！

保羅：嗯，你糟了你，你要用你自己的錢付，這會讓你學到教訓的。

柯絲汀：這不一定是我的錯，讓警察處理吧！

 **慣用語**

1. cut in 切入

He wouldn't stop talking, I couldn't **cut in** at all.

他一直講不停,我找不到機會可以切入。

---

2. freak out 嚇到某人

Tommy jumped out from nowhere, I was totally **freaked out.**

湯米不知道從哪裡跳出來,把我嚇死了!

---

3. blind spot 盲點

I am glad you picked out the error. It was in my **blind spot.**

還好你看到錯誤,我沒有看出來。

---

4. no excuse 別找藉口

There is **no excuse** for the mistake she made. She could have been more careful.

她真的不能為她的失誤找藉口,她本來就應該要仔細一點。

---

5. in a rush 很急

I am **in a rush** every morning. There are so much to do to get ready!

我每天早上都很趕,要準備好很多事才能出門。

---

6. deal with it 面對、處理

I can't **deal with it** right now. I got so much on my plate.

我現在沒有辦法處理，我手上事情很多。

---

7. in deep trouble　很棘手的情況

I got **in deep trouble** with my team leader. He doesn't want me to be in his team anymore.

我跟我的組長鬧翻了，他要把我踢出他的團隊。

---

8. teach someone a lesson　讓某人學到教訓

This would **teach her a lesson.** She can't sit there and daydreaming whole day.

這應該會讓她學到教訓，她不能每天都坐在那裡發呆。

Memo

Unit 58 租車

🌀 前情提要

Oscar 租車到附近的小鎮玩，可是回程卻卡在車陣中，來不及還車。他打電話到租車公司問問看是不是可以不要多付一天錢。

👤 人物角色

- Oscar 租車的客人
- James 租車公司員工

👄 情境對話 ⸺ MP3 58

Oscar: Hi, this is Oscar and I meant to **bring back** the Ford Focus by **close of business** today, but we are **caught in traffic** at the moment, **there is no way** I would **make it** there in time.

奧斯卡：嗨！你好，我本來今天下班之前要把福特的 Focus 還回去，可是我們現在卡在車陣中，我不可能及時趕到。

James: Thanks for letting us know, in that case you will be charged for an extra day.

詹姆士：謝謝你跟我們說，那樣的話你必須多付一天的錢。

Oscar: I know, that's what I am calling for. I will be only a few hours late. Is there some kind of late fee that I can pay instead of paying for the entire day?

奧斯卡：我知道，這也是我打電話給你的理由，我只是遲幾個小時而已，有沒有可能我們付遲到的費用就好？不要收我們一天的錢？

James: Unfortunately, there will be no one here after 5pm.

詹姆士：不好意思，我們 5 點下班之後就沒有人在辦公室了。

Oscar: <u>Is it possible to</u> return the car at your other office at the airport since it's open <u>24/7</u>?

奧斯卡：那我們能不能把車改到你機場的辦公室還，因為是開 24 小時的？

James: <u>That can be arranged</u>, but you still will be paying for the late fee and the location charge.

詹姆士：這我們可以安排，可是你還是要付遲到的費用，還有乙地還車的費用。

慣用語

1. bring back 歸還、拿回去、喚起回憶

Can you **bring this back** to Emily for me please? I borrowed from her a while ago.

你可以幫我把這個拿回去還給艾蜜莉嗎？我前一陣子跟她借的。

---

2. close of business 下班前

I have to hand this in by **close of business** tomorrow. I am still working on it.

這個報告明天下班之前要交，我現在還在寫。

---

3. caught in traffic 塞車

Kenny is **caught in traffic** right now, it would be lucky if he got here before they packed up.

肯尼現在卡在車陣中，如果他能在人家關店之前到就算很好了。

---

4. there is no way 不可能

There is no way Liam is going out with Ariel, I just saw him with someone else last night.

李恩不可能在跟艾瑞兒交往，我昨天晚上才看到他跟別人在一起

---

5. make it 達到、做成

I got a few appointments today, I can't promise you I would **make it** to your party today.

我今天有很多事情要做，我不能保證我一定能去你的派對。

6. in time　及時

Can you drop this off for me at Elaine's desk? I won't get back **in time** to catch her.

你可以幫我把這個放到艾琳的桌上嗎？我來不及在她下班前回到公司。

---

7. is it possible to　可以嗎？

Is it possible to meet up with you tomorrow? I got something to discuss with you.

明天可以跟你見個面嗎？我有事要跟你討論。

---

8. 24/7　全年無休（每週 7 天，每天 24 小時營業）

Some of the gas stations are **24/7**, but not all of them.

有些加油站是開 24 小時的，但不是每一家都是。

Unit 59 分擔油錢

前情提要

　　Rueben 打算從雪梨開車橫跨澳洲到西澳伯斯，他在臉書社群上徵共同分擔油錢的車友，有人打來詢問。

人物角色

- ● Scott 想一起分擔油錢的人
- ● Reuben 貼文徵車伴的人

情境對話　　MP3 59

Scott: Hi, I saw your message that you are looking for someone to **chip in** the petrol to go to Perth. I was wondering when are you going exactly?

史考特：你好，我有看到你的貼文說要找人分擔油錢一起開車到伯斯？我想請問你什麼時候要去？

Reuben: I am **aiming for** getting there before middle of next month, but I am **pretty flexible** if the timing doesn't **suit you.**

魯賓：我計畫下個月中前要到，可是我蠻彈性的，如果時間不適合你的話，我們可以再談。

Scott: How long are you planning to be on the road? I still got work to go to for the next week and half. I can leave on the 10th **if that's ok with you.**

史考特：你打算要開幾天？我目前還要在工作一個半星期。如果你同意的話，我可以 10 號出發。

Reuben: I would prefer to depart earlier, but I guess I can wait for you. I am **in no hurry.**

魯賓：我是希望早一點出發可是沒關係，我可以等你，反正我也不急。

Scott: So the petrol will be 50-50?

史考特：那油錢是一人一半？

Reuben: Well, that's one thing I want to **point out,** I think it would be fair if you could cover 60 and I cover 40 since the car is mine. Would this **work for you**?

魯賓：嗯，我想跟你先說清楚，我覺得既然車也是我出得化的話，我出四成你出六成比較公平，這樣你可以接受嗎？

慣用語

1. chip in　分擔

I am happy to **chip in** for the rent. I don't want to live on your courtesy.

我想給你一點錢當房租，我不好意思讓你一直幫我。

---

2. aim for　預計

I am **aiming for** having this completed by end of the week.

我計畫這星期之前把這個完成。

---

3. pretty flexible　蠻彈性的、還沒有確定

The timing is **pretty flexible,** but I do prefer the morning shifts.

時間是還蠻可以配合的，可是我會比較想要上早班。

---

4. suit someone　適合某人

Let's meet up for lunch tomorrow at 1pm, does it **suit you**?

我們明天一點一起吃中餐好嗎？你可以來嗎？

---

5. if that's ok with someone　如果某人同意的話

If that's ok with you, I would invite Krystal to join us for the meeting.

如果你同意的話，我就請克里斯朵一起來開會。

---

6. in no hurry　不急

I am **in no hurry**. You can take your time.

我不趕時間,你慢慢來就好。

---

7. **point out　講清楚、指出**

I am glad you **pointed it out** for me. I was unsure whether I understood you right.

還好你幫我澄清了,我之前還不太確定我有沒有聽懂你的意思。

---

8. **work for someone　某人可以配合、同意**

Great! That **works for me**, I still got 3 weeks of annual leave, I can take it next month.

太好了,這我可以配合,我還有三個星期的年假,我下個月可以用。

Unit
60 開車被臨檢

前情提要

Carla 剛拿到駕照，對交通規則還不熟悉就到澳洲當背包客，從來沒想過有一天警察會攔她下來臨檢。她看到警車在她後面可是不曉得是要攔她，她最後在路邊停下來，警察下來跟她講話。

人物角色

◉ Jim 交通警察
◉ Carla 開車的觀光客

情境對話　　MP3 60

Jim: I have been signaling you to stop, why didn't you stop?

吉姆：我一直指示你要停下來，你為什麼還一直開？

Carla: Sorry, I wasn't sure you are

卡拉：抱歉我不知道你是

after me.

Jim: You almost **caused an accident** back there, why are you doing 50 at a 70 zone? Are you **under any influence**?

Carla: No, of course not! I thought I was being careful by driving slowly.

Jim: You were **holding up** the traffic, and people were trying to overtake you, that is rather dangerous. Can I have your license please?

Carla: Here you go. This is my international license and passport.

Jim: I suppose the road rules are similar in your country. You got to **keep up with** the traffic and don't slow down **all of a sudden**. Just **be more aware** from now on.

在追我。

吉姆：你知道你剛差點造成車禍嗎？為什麼你在限速 70 的路段開 50？你是嗑藥還是喝酒？

卡拉：不，當然沒有！我只是覺得開慢一點會比較安全。

吉姆：你造成交通堵塞，大家都不斷地超車，這很危險。請給我看你的駕照？

卡拉：拿去，這是我的國際駕照還有護照。

吉姆：我想交通規則在每個國家應該都差不多，你一定要跟上車流，不要突然慢下來，麻煩你從現在開始要多注意。

01 留學生與外派人員

02 上班族

03 異國情侶

04 背包客和觀光客

 慣用語

1. after someone　追逐某人、抓某人

Hello, I am **after Simon**, is he there?

您好，我要找賽門？請問他在嗎？

---

2. cause an accident　釀禍、造成意外

I didn't mean to **cause the accident**, but I was distracted.

我不是故意造成意外的，可是我沒辦法專心。

---

3. under the influence　意識不清（意指喝酒或嗑藥）

She has no idea about what she is doing right now, because she is **under the influence** of alcohol.

她酒喝太多了，根本搞不清楚她在做什麼。

---

4. hold up　阻塞

You better speed up because you are **holding us up.**

你可不可以快一點，因為我們都在等你。

---

5. here you go　給你、拿去

Here you go, these are the documents you asked for.

拿去，這是你要的資料。

---

6. keep up with　跟上

I am trying really hard to **keep up with** you, you work so quickly.

我很努力地要跟上你的速度,你做得好快。

---

7. **all of a sudden**　突然

The weather was quite nice before, but it turned **all of a sudden.**

剛剛天氣還不錯,可是突然間就變天了。

---

8. **be aware**　小心、注意一點

The typhoon is getting stronger. You need to **be aware** of the falling objects on your way to work.

颱風越來越大,你上班途中要小心不要被砸到。

Memo

Unit 61 看醫生沒有保險

🧠 前情提要

　　Miranda 到美國去玩，突然間開始發燒，他想要到當地醫院看醫生可是他沒有買旅遊醫療保險，他不知道該怎麼辦，他硬著頭皮到醫院去問問看。

👤 人物角色

● Miranda 光觀客
● Gayle 護士小姐

💬 情境對話　　　　MP3 61

Miranda: Hello, I am **feeling crook** and I would like to see a doctor.

米蘭達：你好，我不太舒服，我想看醫生。

Gayle: Have you been here before?

蓋兒：你以前來過嗎？

Miranda: No, I am a tourist and I don't have travel insurance, can you tell me roughly how much it would cost?

米蘭達：沒有，我是觀光客，我沒有旅遊保險，你可以跟我說這樣大概要多少錢嗎？

Gayle: To see a doctor would be expensive without the insurance,

蓋兒：看醫生沒有保險是很貴的。

Miranda: I developed a fever last night, and my body is aching, I just don't know what to do.

米蘭達：我咋天晚上開始發燒，我全身痠痛，我不知道要怎麼辦？

Gayle: I would suggest if it is not **life threatening conditions,** you can try to go to the drugstore and get the **over the counter medication**. I mean, you are **heading back** in a few days, aren't you?

蓋兒：我會建議你，如果不是攸關性命的症狀，你可以先去藥局買成藥。我是說，你應該沒幾天就會回國了吧？不是嗎？

Miranda: Thanks, I will **give it a try.** I think it is just a cold, and it will **go away** in a few days.

米蘭達：謝謝，我去試試看，我想應該是感冒，希望它幾天就會好了。

 **慣用語** ----------

1. feeling crook　不舒服、生病了

I am **feeling crook** at the moment. I think I will take the afternoon off.

我現在有點不舒服，我下午要請假。

----

2. have you been here before?　你以前來過嗎？

What a nice restaurant! **Have you been here before**?

這家餐廳好棒喔! 你有來過嗎?

----

3. life threatening conditions　攸關性命的病症

I just found out one of my friend is suffering from a **life threatening condition**.

我剛發現我的一個朋友得了很嚴重的病症。

----

4. over the counter medication　成藥

I have no time to go and see a doctor. I think I will just get some **over the counter medication** for this fever.

我實在沒時間去看醫生，我看我還是去藥局買治發燒的成藥吃吧。

----

5. head back　回去

This is a dead end. We need to **head back.**

這條路不通，我們應該要回頭。

----

6. give it a try　試試看

I am not sure whether this would work, but worth to **give it a**

try.

我不知道這樣行不行得通，可是值得試試看。

---

7. **go away** 治好了、走了

My head is really sore at the moment. It doesn't seem like it will **go away** anytime soon.

現在我的頭很痛，而且我不覺得馬上就會好。

---

8. **better safe than sorry** 後悔就來不及了

I know it takes a long time to get the check-up done, but it is **better safe than sorry.**

我知道做檢查要花很多時間，可是還是情願小心一點，不然後悔就來不及了。

Unit 62 沒趕上飛機

 前情提要

Colin 看錯飛機的時間，趕到機場櫃檯時已經很遲了，他求他們讓他進去

 人物角色

- Colin 遲到的旅客
- Janet 機場地勤人員

情境對話 MP3 62

Colin: Hi, I meant to be on the 12:30 flight to Miami. I am running really late, can you please check me in first?

柯林：您好，我應該是要搭 12:30 的飛機到邁阿密，我已經遲到了，您可不可以讓我先登記？

Janet: **Come with me** to the counter.

珍娜：請跟我到這個櫃台。

Colin: Thanks, **you are my saviour!**

柯林：太感謝了，你真是我的救星！

Janet: Don't **speak too soon**. The gate is about to close in 10 mins, and the check-in for that flight was just closed. I have to check with my supervisor to see if we are allowed to check you in.

珍娜：話別說得太早，登機門在十分鐘就要關了，基本上這班飛機的登記櫃台已經關了，我需要跟我的經理談一下是不是能夠讓你搭這班飛機。

Colin: Please help me out, I really have to make this flight because I **got a cruise booked** in Miami departing tomorrow morning. I know that I am to **be blamed for**. I **should have** been here earlier. But let's just **look at** the situation now.

柯林：求求你幫幫我，我真的必須搭上那班飛機，因為我明天早上還要從邁阿密出發搭郵輪。我知道遲到是我的錯，我真的應該早點來，可是先不要追究，重點是專注在現在的情況。

Janet: I can't say **you are safe** now. I will do my best to help you.

珍娜：我不敢保證一定可以幫你，可是我會盡力。

01 留學生與外派人員

02 上班族

03 異國情侶

04 背包客和觀光客

 **慣用語**

1. come with someone　跟某人來

Mr. Garcia is expecting you, please **come with me** this way.

賈西亞先生已經在等妳了，請跟我這邊走。

---

2. you are my saviour　你是我的救星

Thanks for showing up. **You are my saviour**!

謝謝你趕來，你真是我的救星！

---

3. speak too soon　話說得太早、先別這麼樂觀

I don't want to **speak too soon**, but I do have a feeling that I will get the position.

我不想話説得太早，可是我真的覺得我會得到那份工作。

---

4. got something booked　已經預訂某樣行程

You can't ask me to cancel my leave. I have **got the trip to Hawaii booked**.

你不能叫我取消我的假期，我早就訂好要去夏威夷的行程了。

---

5. to be blamed for　責怪、錯誤

I know he is not the one **to be blamed for.** He is just an executer.

我知道這不是他的錯，他只不過是執行的人而已。

---

6. should have　早應該要

You **should have** been more careful driving in the rain. You could have avoided the accident.

下雨天開車本來就應該要小心一點，這個車禍根本不應該發生。

---

7. **look at** 專注

Let's **look at** this housing project carefully, I think we can make it better by adding a swimming pool here.

讓我們再好好地審視這個建案，我覺得如果在這裡加個游泳池會更好。

---

8. **someone is safe** 某人已經過關了、不用擔心了

I think **Blake is safe** now. The boss realized it is not actually his fault.

我覺得布雷克應該沒事了，老闆知道這不是他的錯。

Unit
63 飯店換房間

前情提要

Anita 入住的這間飯店隔音很差，他一直聽到隔壁房間吵鬧的聲音。他已經打過一次電話到櫃檯抱怨了，可以隔壁還是一直吵。他決定直接下樓來到大廳櫃檯去抱怨。

人物角色

- Anita 入住房客
- Sean 飯店櫃檯

情境對話   MP3 63

Anita: Hi, I am the guest in Room 305, I **made a complaint** **not long ago** to complain the guest next door has been very noisy, but they still

安妮塔：您好，我是 305 房的客人，我剛剛打過電話來抱怨隔壁的房客實在太吵了，可是他們

keep going, **nothing has been done**.

Sean: We are truly sorry. We did **send someone over** to speak to the guests. They promise that they will **keep the volume down.** We will send someone over again shortly.

Anita: I don't know how effective that would be. It is late and I am exhausted, all I want to do is to **get some sleep.** Why don't you look up whether there is another room that you can move me to. I am happy to change the room.

Sean: Sure thing, you can have Room 505. Anything else I can **help you with**?

到現在還在狂歡，沒有人去解決。

西恩：我們真的很抱歉，我們的確有派人過去跟房客勸説了，他們有答應要小聲一點，我們馬上再派人過去。

安妮塔：我不覺得會有什麼用，現在已經很晚了，我也很累了，我只想休息。你可以看看你們有沒有其他房間可以讓我換過去嗎？我情願換房間。

西恩：沒問題，你可以換到 505 號房。還有其他事我們可以幫你服務的嗎？

😮 慣用語

1. **make a complaint** 抱怨

Mary **made a complaint** to the traffic department about the traffic light malfunction during peak hour.

瑪莉向交通部抱怨尖峰時間交通號誌故障的問題。

---

2. **not long ago** 不久之前

I caught up with Sharon **not long ago,** she is doing really well.

我不久之前見過雪倫,她過得很不錯。

---

3. **nothing has been done** 沒有解決、沒有用

I thought they would have fixed the problem by now, but unfortunately **nothing has been done** yet.

我以為那個問題老早就解決了,可是根本沒人去處理。

---

4. **send someone over** 派人過去

Can you please **send the maintenance guy over** please? The bathroom light is not working.

你可以派維修工來嗎?浴室的燈壞掉了。

---

5. **keep the volume down** 小聲一點

Please **keep the volume down**, my kids are asleep.

麻煩你小聲一點,我的小孩們在睡覺。

6. **get some sleep** 睡覺、休息

I can't wait to **get some sleep.** I stayed up so late last night.

我真想趕快睡覺，我昨天很晚才睡。

---

7. **sure thing** 沒問題

It is a **sure thing.** You can count on me.

沒有問題，你可以信任我。

---

8. **help someone with something** 幫忙某人做某事

Can you **help me with moving house** this weekend if you are free?

如果你這週末有空的話可以幫我搬家嗎？

Memo

Unit
64 取消訂房

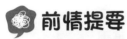

前情提要

Lucas 計畫由大峽谷到拉斯維加斯，原本今天下午就會到拉斯維加斯，可是行程延誤，可能明天才會到。可是飯店已經訂好了，他想問一下是不是可以取消今天的訂房。

人物角色

● Lucas 訂房的旅客
● Jodi 飯店櫃檯

情境對話　　　　　　MP3 64

Lucas: Hello, I got a room **reserved for** today under the name of Lucas Chow, but I am stuck in the Grand Canyon at the moment. I won't get in until tomorrow. My room has been

路卡斯：您好，我今天有訂房，是以路卡斯州的名義。可是我現在卡在大峽谷，我要明天才會到。我的房間已經付清了，可是

pre-paid, but I was wondering wheth-er I could push the booking by a day late.

Jodi: Let me check the details of your booking. Well, unfortunately you booked the **early bird deal** which is non-refundable and non-transferrable. I am afraid that if you don't check in today, you will still be charged.

Lucas: Bul I was **caught out** by the wild weather. The highway is **shut down** and there is nothing I can do.

Jodi: I am really **sorry to hear** that, I will suggest you **bring this up** to your insurance company. Some of travel **insurance policy** would cover it.

我想問問看我是不是可以把日期延後一天在入住？

僑蒂：讓我看一下你的訂房資料，嗯，不好意思你訂的是早鳥專案，是不能退款或轉讓的。如果你今天沒有入住的話，恐怕就浪費了。

路卡斯：可是我是被壞大氣困住，公路都封路了，這不是我能控制的。

僑蒂：真的很抱歉，我只能建議你跟你的保險公司談談，有些旅行保險是有包含這種損失的。

01 留學生與外派人員

02 上班族

03 異國情侶

04 背包客和觀光客

275

🐤 慣用語

1. **reserve for** 預約給某人

Can you please **reserve a table for** me and boyfriend for tomorrow night at 7 pm please?

麻煩你幫我跟我男朋友預約明天晚上七點嗎？

---

2. **pre-paid** 預付

I got a **pre-paid** SIM card here, so you can reach me with my Australian number.

我在這裡有辦預付卡，你可以打我澳洲的電話給我。

---

3. **early bird deal** 早鳥專案

I got a really good price with the **early bird deal.**

我買到早鳥專案的優惠價格。

---

4. **caught out by something** 被困住

I got **caught out by** the unexpected traffic jam, otherwise I would have been here much earlier.

要不是遇上意外的塞車，我早就來了。

---

5. **shut down** 關閉

Even if the power **shuts down,** we still got the emergency generator.

就算停電，我們還是有緊急供電器。

6. sorry to hear that 聽到這個消息很難過

I am really **sorry to hear that** your brother lost his job last week.

聽到你哥哥上星期被裁員的消息很為你難過。

---

7. bring something up 跟某人討論

I have been wanting to **bring this up** with you for quite some time.

我很早以前就想要跟你討論這個問題了。

---

8. insurance policy 保險的內容

I am unsure about my **insurance policy**. I need to check it again.

我不太確定我的保險內容，我需要再看一下。

Unit 65 不滿意旅行團的服務

 前情提要

Heather 參加了兩天一夜的行程，雖然是包吃包住，可是他覺得食宿的品質都很差，他想向旅行社反應。

 人物角色

● Heather 參加旅行團的團友
● Maurice 旅行社的導遊

 情境對話 MP3 65

Heather: I like the tourist attractions we visited, but in general I think there is definitely **room for improvement.**

海瑟：我喜歡我們去的那些景點，可是整體來說是還有很大的改善空間。

Maurice: How so?

毛利斯：怎麼說呢？

Heather: You got to admit it, the hotel that we stayed last night is so dated, and the mattress is so uncomfortable.

Maurice: I know the hotel **can do with** a makeover, but it is still functional.

Heather: Don't get me started on the food. It is so basic, even our **so-call** deluxe seafood BBQ last night. There were only **handful of** the shrimps and some squid rings which is barely enough **to go around.** There is nothing fancy about it about this tour, you should rename it a budget tour. I know I signed up for a **mid-range** comfort tour, but this definitely is more a budget one.

海瑟：你必須要承認，昨天晚上我們待的那個飯店好舊，而且床墊好不舒服。

毛利斯：我知道那間飯店外觀需要整修一下，可是還是可以使用。

海瑟：更不要說餐點了，全部都好基本，就連昨天晚上所謂的海鮮總匯燒烤也只不過有幾隻蝦跟魷魚圈，根本都不夠吃。整趟旅程下來沒什麼特別的，應該更名為廉價旅行團。我知道，我參加的是中等的舒適團，可是這感覺上就像廉價團。

 慣用語

1. room for improvement　有改善的空間

I tried really hard to finish this piece for you, but I understand there is **room for improvement.**

我很努力的把這個作品完成，可是我瞭解還是有改善的空間。

---

2. you got to admit it　承認吧

You got to admit it. Your boyfriend is a bit fat.

承認吧！妳男朋友真的是有點肥。

---

3. can do with　需要

I am so sleepy now, I **can do with** a nap.

我好睏，我真需要小睡一下。

---

4. don't get me started　不是我要抱怨…

Don't get me started on his fashion sense, who wears sandals with socks!

不是我要抱怨他的品味，有誰會穿襪子配涼鞋的！

---

5. so-called　所謂的

I tried the **so-called** fast effective diet, but it didn't work.

我試過所謂的快速減肥飲食，可是沒有用。

---

6. handful of　一把、一點

Apparently a **handful of** nuts a day is very good for you.

每天吃一點堅果類，其實對健康很有助益。

---

7. **to go around**　分享、分著吃

I prepared lot of fruits, I am sure it will be enough **to go around.**

我準備了很多水果，我覺得一定夠大家吃。

---

8. **mid-range**　中階的、中級的

I am looking for something a bit **mid-range,** I don't want the budget stuff.

我想要找等級稍微高一點的，我不要廉價的束西。

Memo

Unit
66 迷路

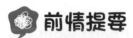
前情提要

Roger 看著地圖試著要找大都會博物館，他在附近找來找去都找不到，決定要問人。

人物角色

● Roger 問路的觀光客
● Eason 當地人

情境對話 `MP3 66`

Roger: Hello, I am having trouble to find the Metropolitan museum, would you be able to point out the **general direction** for me please?

羅傑：你好，我一直找不到大都會博物館，你可以跟我說大概的方向在哪裡嗎？

Eason: Metropolitan museum!? You

伊森：大都會博物館？！

are **a long way away** from it. I guess you got off the subway too early. It will take you at least half an hour to get there **by foot.**

Roger: Right, what would you suggest me?

Eason: I think the easiest way would be **cut through** central park until you **run into** 5th Ave then turn right. You should **have no trouble** finding it once you are on 5th Ave.

Roger: Thanks for your help, I have been **running around in circles** for the past twenty minutes trying to **find my way**. I should have asked someone sooner.

還很遠唉！我猜你應該是太早下地鐵了，如果走過去也至少要半個小時。

羅傑：那你會建議我怎麼做？

伊森：我覺得最容易的方式就是切過中央公園，一直到第五大道，在第五大道右轉。如果你到了第五大道，你就一定找的到。

羅傑：謝謝你的幫忙，我已經原地打轉二十分鐘了還找不到。我應該早點問人的。

01 留學生與外派人員

02 上班族

03 異國情侶

04 背包客和觀光客

 慣用語 ------------------------

1. general direction　大概的方向

To maximise profits would be the **general direction** for the next 6 months.

增加盈餘將會是接下來半年的大方向。

---

2. long way away　離的很遠

A managerial role seems **long way away,** but if you work hard, you will get there one day.

經理的職位看似很遙遠，可是如果你努力的話，總有一天會達成。

---

3. by foot　用走的

Don't be too surprised. I actually got here **by foot**

不要太驚訝，我其實是走路來的。

---

4. cut through　切過去

You will get there much if you **cut through** the bushes.

如果你穿過這些樹叢，你很快就會到了。

---

5. run into　遇到

Guess who I **run into** in New York? Brad Pitt!

你猜我在紐約遇到誰？布萊德彼特！

---

6. have no trouble　沒有問題

Once you got your degree, you would **have no trouble**

getting a job.

等你大學畢業之後，要找工作絕對沒問題。

---

7. **run around in circles** **一直找不到、原地打轉**

I am **running around in circles**, where a hell is the book store?

我一直找來找去，那家書店到底在哪裡？

---

8. **find someone's way** **找方向**

I have been trying to **find my way**, I am feeling lost in life.

我一直思考我到底想做什麼，我有點迷失方向。

Memo

Unit
67
錯過該搭的車

 前情提要

　　Maggie 在青年旅館認識 Sandy，兩個人並不熟，可是約好明天要一起去環球影城，可是 Sandy 動作太慢，錯過了原本要搭的巴士，兩個人吵起來了。

 人物角色

- Maggie 背包客
- Sandy 在青年旅館認識的背包客

 情境對話　　　 MP3 67

Maggie: Look what happened! We just missed the bus!

瑪姬：你看看！我們真的錯過巴士了！

Sandy: That's ok, I am sure the next one will be here soon.

珊蒂：沒關係，我想下一班應該馬上就來了。

Maggie: I think you really need to **manage your timing a bit better.**

瑪姬：我覺得你應該善用你的時間。

Sandy: What do you mean?

珊蒂：你是什麼意思？

Maggie: Well, if it wasn't for you **taking your time** curling your hair, we would have been on the bus **as we speak.**

瑪姬：嗯，如果不是因為你還在那邊慢慢捲頭髮，我們早就在巴士上了。

Sandy: Missing a bus is just a **minor issue,** but I really don't appreciate you criticising me like that. You can go to Universal studio **on your own**, I much prefer to **spend time with** my hair curler.

珊蒂：沒搭上巴士只不過是件小事，但我真的很不喜歡你這樣批評我。你可以自己去環球影城，我情願回去慢慢捲我的頭髮。

Maggie: I don't mean to **offend you**, but I only a have a few days here in LA. I really want to **make the most of it.**

瑪姬：我不是故意要得罪你，可是我在洛杉磯只有幾天的時間，我真的想好好利用。

 慣用語

1. **manage something better** 將某件事安排得更好

I wish I can **manage my workload better,** I can't keep doing overtime night after night.

我希望我可以把我的工作量安排得更好,我總不能一直不停的加班下去。

---

2. **take someone's time** 請某人慢慢來

I can't believe she is still **taking her time** to get ready, we really need to leave now.

真不敢相信她還在慢慢打扮,我們現在就應該要出門了!

---

3. **as we speak** 此刻、當下

My sister is on the flight over **as we speak.**

我妹妹此刻正搭著飛機過來。

---

4. **minor issue** 小問題

This is a **minor issue,** I can fix it with a little adjustment.

這只是小問題,我稍微調整一下就好了。

---

5. **on someone's own** 靠某人自己

Don't worry, I can do this **on my own.**

不用擔心,我可以自己處理。

---

6. **spend time with** 花時間陪某人或物

I haven't been able to **spend time with** my families much

lately.

我最近沒什麼機會陪家人。

---

7. **offend someone**　得罪某人

I apologize for what I said. That was not my intention to **offend you.**

我對我説的話很抱歉，我不是有意要得罪你。

---

8. **make the most of it**　善加利用、好好珍惜

Going to the America is a wonderful opportunity. You should **make the most of It.**

去美國是個很棒的機會，你要好好珍惜

Memo

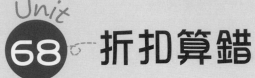

Unit
68 折扣算錯

前情提要

Melinda 在機場拿了一本當地的旅遊廣告手冊,她拿手冊上的折價券到餐廳吃東西,可是結帳的時候餐廳忘了給他們折扣。

人物角色

● Troy 餐廳結帳人員
● Melinda 用完餐的觀光客

情境對話　　MP3 68

Troy: The total **comes to** 51.75 dollars.

特洛伊:總共是 51.75 美金。

Melinda: Well, it **doesn't seem right.** My **combo** is 25 and the BBQ ribs **on its own** is 25. That should be

瑪琳達:嗯,好像不太對,我的套餐是 25 元,單點碳烤肋排是 25 元。

50 dollars, and we got a coupon for 10 percent off the total bill. I don't understand how did you get the total of 51.75?

Troy: Yes, we did take 10 percent off, but there is a 15 percent service charge applied to the total bill.

Melinda: Where did it say that?

Troy: That's mentioned in the **fine print.**

Melinda: Right, I didn't realize that, that's a lot!

Troy: This must be your first time in the US. You will **get your head around** it pretty soon.

Melinda: I don't like the rule but **what can I do!**

我有一張總價打九折的折價券，這樣怎麼會是 51.75 元呢？

特洛伊：是的，我們已經把折扣算進去了，可是還要另外加一成五的服務費。

瑪琳達：怎麼會，我沒有看到。

特洛伊：明細裡有註明。

瑪琳達：是嗎？我怎麼沒發現，這金額其實很大。

特洛伊：這你一定是第一次到美國。你很快就會知道的。

瑪琳達：我並不喜歡這個規定，但我又能怎樣呢？

01 留學生與外派人員

02 上班族

03 異國情侶

04 背包客和觀光客

 **慣用語** ------------------

1. come to 總金額是…

How much did the dinner **come to**?

晚餐一共多少錢？

---

2. not seem right 好像不太對

I can't tell you what is wrong with him, but he just **doesn't seem right.**

我沒辦法跟你說他有什麼問題，可是他看起來就是怪怪的。

---

3. combo 套餐

Can I make my burger a **combo** please?

我的漢堡可以加套餐嗎？

---

4. on its own 單點

I don't want fries. I just want the drink **on its own.**

我不要薯條，我只要一杯飲料。

---

5. where did it say that? 哪裡有註明？

I didn't realised the bank charges a fee every time I made an withdraw, **where did it say that?**

我不知道我每次領錢銀行都會扣手續費，有註明嗎？

---

6. fine print 明細、詳細說明

You must read the **fine print** carefully, there are lots of hidden catches.

你一定要仔細看説明的部分，有很多隱藏的陷阱。

---

7. **get someone's head around it　接受**

I can't get used to the recent changes happening in the company. I need some time to **get my head around it.**

我還沒辦法接受最近公司一連串的改變，我需要一點時間來習慣。

---

8. **what can I do　我又能怎樣、無可奈何**

They decided to let me go, **what can I do!**

他們要把我辭退，我又能怎樣呢？

Memo

293

Unit 69 機場退稅

 前情提要

Marcie 到退稅櫃台辦退稅，可是退稅櫃台人員要求要看物品，但是物品早已打包放在行李中。

 人物角色

● Marcie 準備離境的觀光客
● Joe 退稅櫃台人員

💬 情境對話 ┈┈┈┈┈ MP3 69

Marcie: Hi, here is my receipt for the refund.

瑪西：嗨！這是我要申請退稅的收據。

Joe: Thanks, can I take a look at the items please?

喬：謝謝，我可以看一下物品嗎？

Marcie: Oh no, I don't <u>**have them with me**</u>. I packed them all in my <u>**check-in.**</u>

Joe: We actually need to see the things you bought to <u>**verify against**</u> the receipt.

Marcie: I am so sorry, I was not aware that I need to present them to you. I got my computer to carry and there is <u>**not much room**</u> left in my <u>**carry-on**</u>. Plus, <u>**one of the**</u> items is 100ml perfume, I am not allowed to have it as carry-on anyway. I <u>**swear to God**</u> I am a genuine tourist, I was just not aware of the rules. Please <u>**make an exception**</u> for me this time. I will remember it in the future.

瑪西：喔！糟糕！我沒有隨身帶著，我全部包在行李裡面。

喬：我們需要核對一下收據和商品。

瑪西：我真的很抱歉,我不知道我需要拿商品給你看。我有一台電腦要帶,所以隨身行李沒什麼位子的。還有,我其中的一個商品是一瓶 100ml 的香水,我也沒辦法放進隨身行李裡。我發誓我真的只是單純的觀光客,我不清楚退稅的規定,是不是可以請您這次放我一馬,我以後一定會記得的。

 **慣用語**

1. have something with me　隨身帶著

Is it possible to borrow 50 dollars off you? I didn't **have my wallet with me.**

可以跟你借五十塊嗎？我忘了帶錢包。

---

2. check-in　登記

The **check-in** counter closes approximately 40 minutes before the departure.

登機櫃台大概起飛前四十分鐘就會關閉。

---

3. one of somethings　某物的其中之一

One of my friends makes really good cake.

我的一個好朋友很會烤蛋糕。

---

4. verify against　核對、查閱

The total amount doesn't seem right. I will **verify against** the accountant's record tomorrow.

這個總金額好像不太對，我明天再跟會計師的紀錄對一下。

---

5. not much room　沒什麼空間

The room is rather small. There is **not much room** left once we put the bed in.

這個房間很小，我們把床放進去之後就沒什麼位子了。

6. **carry-on** 隨身行李

You better check with the airline about your allowance for **carry-on**.

你最好跟航空公司確認一下手提行李的規定。

---

7. **swear to God** 對天發誓

I **swear to God** I didn't do this, I was the first one to leave the office.

我對天發誓不是我做的,我是第一個離開辦公室的人。

---

8. **make an exception** 高抬貴手、幫幫忙

Thanks for **making an exception** for me. I really appreciate it.

謝謝你放我一馬,我真的很感謝。

Unit 70 護照弄丟重新申請

 前情提要

傑米在美國發現護照被偷了，要重新申請需要提供當地的報案證明，證明需要到警察局去申請。

 人物角色

- Jamie 觀光客
- Rhys 警員

情境對話 ······ MP3 70

Jamie: Hello, I would like to **launch a police report** about some stolen property.

傑米：您好，我想要報案，我的東西被偷了。

Rhys: I can sort it out for you. Just need to **get a few details off you**.

瑞斯：我可以幫你，只是需要你的一些資料，可以

Can you **talk me through** about what happened?

告訴我發生什麼事嗎？

Jamie: Someone **cut my backpack open** and stole my passport and camera, and I am **not exactly sure** when it happened, but I can tell you the last time I saw my camera was about lunch time in Times square.

傑米：有人把我的背包割開，偷了我的護照還有相機。我不確定是什麼時候發生的，可是我可以跟你說我最後一次看到我的相機是大概中午的時候，在時代廣場。

Rhys: Ok, I must tell you **the chance is slim** for the items to be found, but if you can fill out this form, then I will **put it through** to our system. Your report number is TR00201653.

瑞斯：好的，我必須老實跟你說東西不太可能找的回來，可是如果你可以填完這張表格，我可以輸入在我們的系統內建檔，你的報案號碼是：TR002 01653。

Jamie: Can I have a **hard copy** of the report please? I need it for the embassy to issue a passport replacement for me.

傑米：可以印一張報案紀錄出來給我嗎？我需要紙本報告來申請新的護照。

01 留學生與外派人員

02 上班族

03 異國情侶

04 背包客和觀光客

慣用語

1. launch a report 報案

You need to **launch an official report** before we can do anything.

你必須要先正式報案我們才能處理。

---

2. get something off someone 跟某人拿取某物

If you are done with the report, can I **get it off you** please?

如果你報告看完了，可以換我看嗎？

---

3. talk someone through 跟某人敘述細節

Talk me through what happened between you and Tony. I don't understand why he is so upset with you.

跟我詳細說明你跟湯尼之間發生什麼事，我不知道他為什麼這麼生你的氣。

---

4. cut something open 把某物割開

I can't open this gift wrapping. I think I am going to **cut it open**.

我打不開這個禮物包裝紙。我還是把它割開好了。

---

5. not exactly sure 不太確定

Shelly is **not exactly sure** whether Clive is right for her.

雪莉不太確定克萊夫是不是真的適合她。

6. the chance is slim 　機會渺茫

I really wish Dave could ask me out, but I know **the chance is slim.**

我真的好希望戴夫會想約我出去，可是我知道不太可能。

---

7. put something through 　輸入、處理

Take your time choosing the main dish. I can **put your drink order through** first.

你可以慢慢看要吃什麼主餐。我可以先處理你要的飲料。

---

8. hard copy 　紙本、印出來

Can you print out a **hard copy** for me please? I would like to make notes as I read.

可以麻煩你幫我印出來嗎？我想要一邊看一邊做註記。

篇章回顧

🌀 精選慣用語

1. **not have a clue** 不懂、不知道

She **doesn't have a clue** about how to entering the data into the system.

她完全不知道怎樣輸入資料到這個系統裡。

---

2. **a quick word** 簡單談一下

Let me know if you have a minute, I just want to have **a quick word** with you.

如果你有空讓我知道，我有事想跟你簡單講一下。

---

3. **doesn't add up** 不清不楚、對不起來

I don't think Rose is telling the truth, what she said just **doesn't add up.**

我覺得羅莎沒有講實話，她所說的細節都對不起來。

---

4. **screw someone over** 整某人、搞砸某人的計畫

He really **screwed me over,** he left half way without telling anyone.

我被他害死了！他事情做到一半，沒有跟任何人說就消失了。

---

5. **better safe than sorry** 後悔就來不及了

I know it takes a long time to get the check-up done, but it is **better safe than sorry.**

我知道做檢查要花很多時間，可是還是情願小心一點，不然後悔就來不及了。

---

6. **speak too soon** 話說得太早、先別這麼樂觀

I don't want to **speak too soon**, but I do have a feeling that I will get the position.

---

7. **swear to God** 對天發誓

I **swear to God** I didn't do this, I was the first one to leave office.

我對天發誓不是我做的，我是第一個離開辦公室的人。

---

8. **make an exception** 高抬貴手、幫幫忙

Thanks for **making an exception** for me. I really appreciate it.

謝謝你放我一馬，我真的很感謝。

Learn Smart! 064

冤家英語 (附 MP3)

作　　者	陳幸美
發 行 人	周瑞德
執行總監	齊心瑀
企劃編輯	陳韋佑
校　　對	編輯部
封面構成	高鍾琪

內頁構成	菩薩蠻數位文化有限公司
印　　製	大亞彩色印刷製版股份有限公司
初　　版	2016 年 9 月
定　　價	新台幣 360 元
出　　版	倍斯特出版事業有限公司
電　　話	(02) 2351-2007
傳　　真	(02) 2351-0887
地　　址	100 台北市中正區福州街 1 號 10 樓之 2
E - m a i l	best.books.service@gmail.com
網　　址	www.bestbookstw.com

港澳地區總經銷	泛華發行代理有限公司
地　　址	香港新界將軍澳工業邨駿昌街 7 號 2 樓
電　　話	(852) 2798-2323
傳　　真	(852) 2796-5471

國家圖書館出版品預行編目資料

冤家英語 / 陳幸美著. -- 初版. -- 臺北
市：倍斯特，2016.09 面； 公分. --
(Learn smart! ; 64)
ISBN 978-986-92855-6-8(平裝附光碟片)
1. 英語 2. 會話
　　805.188　　　　　　　　105014312